D0977305

SCREAM SITE

Scream Site is published in 2018 by Capstone Editions,
A Capstone Imprint
1710 Roe Crest Drive
North Mankato, Minnesota 56003
www.mycapstone.com

Text © 2018 Capstone Editions

Library of Congress Cataloging-in-Publication Data
Names: Ireland, Justina, author.
Title: Scream Site / by Justina Ireland.
Description: North Mankato, Minnesota : Capstone Editions., an imprint of
Capstone Editions, [2018] | Series: Capstone editions | Summary: Future
investigative reporter Sabrina, fourteen, researches a popular website where
people post horror videos, hoping to prove they are not as real as they seem
until her sister, a big fan of the site, disappears.
Identifiers: LCCN 2018004892 (print) | LCCN 2018011924 (ebook) | ISBN
9781630791032 (reflowable ePub) | ISBN 9781630791025 (hardcover)
Subjects: | CYAC: Investigative reporting—Fiction. | Reporters and reporting—
Fiction. | Horror films—Fiction. | Video recordings—Fiction. | Web sites—
Fiction. | Sisters—Fiction. | Missing children—Fiction.
Classification: LCC PZ7.I6274 (ebook) | LCC PZ7.I6274 Scr 2018 (print) | DDC
[Fic]—dc23
LC record available at https://lccn.loc.gov/201800489

Editor: Kristen Mohn
Designer: Kay Fraser

Illustration by Brann Garvey

Printed in the United States of America.
366

SCREAM SITE

BY JUSTINA IRELAND

CAPSTONE EDITIONS
a capstone imprint

CHAPTER ONE

"So, what do you think? Should I go with 'Taco Tuesday Is a Day Made of Lies' or 'Football Team Organizes Book Drive for Local Library'? Those are my two best stories, and I've narrowed it down to them. I think. I'm actually not sure."

Sabrina Sebastian leaned back in her chair and waited for her best friend, Evelyn Chao, to respond. They sat in Lou's Brews, the only coffee shop in Port Riverton. It was the hangout spot for everyone in town. From the wooden booths and red tables to the wood-paneled walls covered with pictures by local artists, Lou's was one of Sabrina's favorite places.

No matter where she was in Port Riverton, it seemed she could smell Lou's fresh bread baking, and there was nothing like Lou's coffee. The shop served the best sandwiches, and it was known far and wide for its crab salad, a specialty in Maryland, where everything was crab something or other.

Evelyn and Sabrina had a table reserved for them every day after school, if they wanted, on account of Sabrina's older sister, Faith, working there as a barista. It was one of the few nice things Faith did for her these days. Most of the time, Faith just ignored Sabrina, but that wasn't unexpected. Sabrina had learned that in high school, everyone had a habit of ignoring freshmen, especially juniors like Faith.

Usually Sabrina and Evelyn pretended to do homework but spent more time watching the comings and goings of people than actually studying. Not today, though. Sabrina was working on her application packet for the *Daily Sun* summer internship program. It was something she'd wanted to do ever since she was small, and this was the first year Sabrina was old enough to apply. It was a huge deal when her mom agreed that she should go for it, and Sabrina would do everything in her power to make sure she didn't waste such an opportunity.

Sabrina tapped her pen against her lips and considered the two articles before her. "I think my exposé about the meat content in the school lunches shows that I'm the kind of reporter who can follow a lead to the end, even one that is kind of gross. But the charity drive story shows that I understand that even good news can be interesting. It doesn't have to be all scandal and tragedy." She'd cut the stories out of the school newspaper, the *Mount Clare Chronicle*, and was trying to decide which one to include with her packet. The application deadline for the *Daily Sun* summer internship program was just a few weeks away.

Evelyn groaned. "Why exactly are you applying for an internship, Sabrina? We're freshman. We're supposed to be having fun and figuring stuff out, not planning our futures! I kind of think fourteen is too young for an internship. I mean, it's bad enough my family makes me work at the store, and here you are volunteering for *more* work. Aren't internships something that college kids do?"

Sabrina tucked a strand of her curly brown hair behind her ear and leaned forward. Her brown cheeks were flushed, and her dark eyes sparkled with excitement. What Evelyn saw as work, Sabrina saw as a chance at something. "Maybe, but it doesn't even seem like work to me. Just think how exciting it would be to spend all summer at the newspaper—shadowing reporters, reading the breaking news coming off the wire!"

"Getting coffee for everyone and being stuck at the copy machine all day . . . ," Evelyn said and blew her straight bangs off her face. Usually she had a stripe of some color or other in her dark hair, but today the stripe was just bleached blond as she debated her next color option. Evelyn was just trying to figure out what would scandalize her grandparents the most. They had emigrated to the United States from China a long time ago and were very old fashioned in some ways. They owned Port Riverton's only grocery store, and Evelyn spent most of her free time there, helping out, along with her parents and brother, Tony. The colored streak in Evelyn's hair was one of many small rebellions. That rebellious "streak" was one of the reasons Sabrina adored her friend. She sometimes wished she could be as wild and carefree as Evelyn. But Sabrina was the cautious one, and even though that might not be exciting, it kept her out of trouble— and helped keep Evelyn out of trouble as well.

"Look, Sabrina, no offense, but these stories are boring," Evelyn continued. "No one wants to read about school lunches or charitable football players. You need a story that will get people to sit up and pay attention. Like this . . . " Evelyn scrolled through her phone before holding it up for Sabrina to see. On the screen was a story from one of the celebrity gossip websites Evelyn loved: HOTTEST COUPLE IN

HOLLYWOOD BREAKS UP—DIVORCE NEXT? the headline screamed.

Sabrina groaned. "That isn't news."

Evelyn's eyes widened. "Are you kidding? It most definitely is! This story has over two million clicks. Adam and Leatrice breaking up is the biggest thing to happen since that weird viral photo of Hayley Anderson eating the cake and crying." Evelyn began to swipe through photos, muttering under her breath about Sabrina's lack of interest in "current events."

Sabrina sighed. "I don't want to write about Hollywood breakups. That just isn't my thing. But you're right, the stories I have here totally make me sound like a kid. I need something more adult, some sort of inside scoop into a real issue that'll make me stand out."

Evelyn nodded along to Sabrina's words, but her eyes never left her phone. She just kept scrolling through articles, a slight frown on her face. Sabrina waited a moment before smacking her hand down on the table. "Ev, are you even listening to me?"

"I am! I was looking for something. Here." Evelyn held up her phone again so that Sabrina could read the screen. It was a different story from the same site, and the picture was of a woman screaming, her eyes wide with fright. SCREAM SITE WORTH SCREAMING ABOUT? the headline read.

"I can send it to you. This is what you should write about," Evelyn said, thumbs moving as she scrolled through the story. "It's this trending website, Scream Site. It was created by Hollywood types who make horror movies, and they're giving out a huge prize for the video that has the most likes and shares—the most 'screams'—at the end of the year. Here, look," Evelyn said, showing Sabrina a website landing page.

Sabrina stuck out her tongue. "A website? That's hardly news," she said. She'd barely gotten a glimpse of a page covered in shades of black and red before Evelyn pulled her phone back.

"No, but what makes it weird is that there are rumors that girls have actually gone missing after posting videos on there. Creepy, right?"

Sabrina shrugged. "I guess. But Internet rumors aren't exactly news."

"Not usually, but one of the girls who went missing was supposed to be from around here. See, you could take sort of a local angle on a national story."

"National *rumor*," Sabrina corrected her.

"Just check out the story. It might be worth your while."

Sabrina sighed. "I don't know. I doubt Mrs. Wembley would be interested in it. She thinks that journalism should be serious, not sensational."

"Ugh, that woman is harsh. Did I tell you she

gave me a B on my *Romeo and Juliet* assignment? Just because I called the play depressing. Which it totally is!" Mid-complaint, Evelyn suddenly froze, her eyes locked on the door of Lou's Brews. "Oh my god," she breathed.

"What? What's happening?" Sabrina asked, turning around in her seat.

"It's Asher Grey. Light of my life, most beauteous of boys," Evelyn said, pretending to swoon.

Sabrina rolled her eyes and turned back around. "I'm having a crisis here, and you're staring at unachievable junior boys."

"Oh, Asher totally isn't my type. But that doesn't mean I can't appreciate his physical qualities. Look at that golden hair, those eyes as blue as a storm-tossed sea."

"Would a storm-tossed sea be blue?" Sabrina asked.

Evelyn shrugged. "I don't know, it just sounded good. Anyway, he's gone now. OK, I sent you the link for that Scream Site story. Check it out. Since one of the girls was from around here, it'd be good for the *Daily Sun* thing, I think." Evelyn stood and started to pack up her stuff. "I have to get going, it's almost five. Tony isn't home this week so I have to cover for him at the store."

Sabrina stood as well. "Yeah, I should get going

too. I have a paper to write for history and a new article due to Mrs. Wembley soon. I need to find something to pitch to her."

"Write about Scream Site," Evelyn said, standing up from the table and pushing in her chair. "Seriously, it's all anyone can talk about right now. Maybe you can use it for both Wembley's assignment and the internship application. And you can write about something that isn't serious for a change. Try bold and crazy for once!" Evelyn waved and made her way out of Lou's Brews.

Sabrina picked up her almost empty smoothie and drank the rest of it. The café was beginning to fill as the early dinner crowd came in, mothers with strollers and harried-looking career people grabbing a quick bite to eat. Faith caught Sabrina's eye as she was ringing up a customer. Faith made a quick head motion, almost as though she was trying to get her attention. Sabrina smiled at her sister, but Faith didn't return the expression. Instead, she frowned.

After she had finished with her customer, Faith beelined over to the table, a dish rag and bottle of spray cleaner in her hand. Faith had the same dark brown skin as Sabrina, but she was taller and wore her hair in a sleek, chin-length bob. Sabrina's own hair was a wild mass of curls that hung past her shoulders. She sometimes imagined what it would be like to style her hair like her sister's. She'd tried straightening it once, but the hours of work just hadn't seemed worth it.

As Faith approached, she wore the same half frown that had seemed pinned to her face ever since their father's death from a heart attack last year. Sabrina sat up a little straighter. "Hey, is something wrong?"

"Are you going to be much longer? It's getting close to dinnertime," Faith said, pulling at her silver necklace and eyeing the leftover plates and cups from Sabrina and Evelyn's snack.

"Oh no, I'm done. Why? Did you want to go grab something to eat?"

"No, I have another two hours on my shift. But if you're done, you should get going. Lou doesn't like for kids to hang out too long, and if he finds out I save you and Evelyn a table every day, I could get in trouble."

Sabrina tried not to let her disappointment show as she stood. "Oh. Sorry. Yeah, I'm heading out now. I guess I'll see you at home?"

"Sure," Faith said, but she was already focused on the table, clearing the dishes and wiping it down, erasing any trace of Sabrina and Evelyn's visit.

Sabrina put on her backpack, looked one last time at her sister, then headed home.

CHAPTER TWO

Port Riverton was a small town with a main street and not much else. Lou's Brews sat next to an insurance office and across the street from Evelyn's family's store. The library and police station were just a few blocks down from Lou's. A few blocks beyond that, through a neighborhood of matching houses, were the high school and middle school. Most everyone Sabrina knew lived in town, but not her family. They lived in a development a couple of miles away, which felt like a hundred miles when it was cold and dark.

After she had made her way down the country road to her house, Sabrina parked her bike in the garage, feeling a bit trepidatious and a little lonely. Dark windows greeted her like vacant eye sockets. This wasn't unusual, but just because it was expected didn't stop her from feeling kind of scared.

When her father was alive, she would come home to a brightly lit house, with him watching television or making dinner or preparing for the night shift as a detective with the Port Riverton Police Department. But now that he was gone, there wasn't anyone around when Sabrina got home. Faith was rarely home because she seemed to take as many hours at Lou's Brews as she could. And if she wasn't at Lou's, she was hanging out with her friends or practicing for the dance team. It was like Faith kept herself super busy to keep her mind off other things. And their mom was a nurse who worked extra hours to pay the bills, often pulling back-to-back shifts. Tonight she wouldn't be home until seven. So it was just Sabrina all by herself, as usual.

She didn't normally mind too much, but tonight it felt eerie to enter the quiet house. Maybe she was still thinking about what Evelyn had said about the website. What was it again? Terror Site? No, Scream Site. Girls going missing after using a website sounded like every dumb cautionary tale she'd ever been told. Yet the thought of it made Sabrina feel nervous, like there were murderers around every corner.

She gave herself a mental shake and laughed at her silliness. There was no way any of this was true. This was what she got for listening to Evelyn's wild stories.

And yet, Sabrina still felt unsettled, a chill running down her spine as she crossed the threshold from the garage into the kitchen. Right away she noticed that the stove-top clock was out. She always checked the time as soon as she walked in. The sight of the blank clock stopped her in the doorway.

Was the power out again?

She stood in the kitchen and flipped the light switch, but it did nothing. The breaker needed to be flipped, which meant a trip to the basement. Sabrina sighed out loud into the growing darkness. She hated the basement. It wasn't actually all that creepy, but it was definitely dark. When her dad was still alive, he was usually in charge of resetting the breaker whenever it tripped. With him gone, it was left to whoever discovered the power outage.

And unfortunately, today that was Sabrina.

She gave her eyes a moment to adjust to the inky interior before journeying toward the closet and grabbing the flashlight. The stairs to the basement were near the foyer, and even with the flashlight on, Sabrina's heart pounded in her chest. She hated the dark, and especially hated being alone in the dark.

She ran down the stairs and quickly reset the breaker like her mother had taught her. Then she ran back up the stairs and through the living room, flipping light switches as she went. She turned on every single one, hoping the golden light would banish the unsettled feeling that had taken her over. It didn't.

"Stop being ridiculous, Sebastian," she muttered to herself. Still, her heart was in her ears, loud as a bass drum as she ran up to her room, grabbed her laptop, and sprinted back downstairs to the living room.

Sabrina opened her laptop and checked her email. Evelyn had said she would send her a link, and even though Sabrina could've read the email on her phone, she liked working on her laptop better. It would be easier to research whether whatever Evelyn had sent her was true. Evelyn loved conspiracies, and she was always sending Sabrina things like "Shark Boy Captured by Fishing Boat" or "Thirty-Two Pictures that Prove the Earth Is Flat." Sabrina wasn't sure how many of these things her friend believed, but Sabrina secretly enjoyed getting to the truth behind each story and debunking it. It was why she wanted to be an investigative journalist: Looking for answers was a challenge.

Sabrina found the email and opened the link. She quickly scanned the article:

IS SCREAM SITE TOO REAL?

Parents have complained recently about a new website known as Scream Site. Hosted and founded by the Scarapelli Brothers, directors of such horror movies as *Your Blood Is Mine* and *Hotel of Death 1-4*, the Scarapellis state that they founded the site in order to find "the next generation of horror movie directors and talent." Users are asked to post their own videos as well as vote on their favorites, with the daily top ten posted on the main landing page of the site. The competition is scheduled to run on an annual basis, and the user with the most votes each year wins an all-expenses paid trip to California as well as the chance to have their idea made into a movie by the Scarapellis.

But some have complained that the site is too real, showing footage of what appear to be actual kidnappings, assault, and torture.

"My sister is missing and the police refuse to investigate the video that was posted around that time. But I know what my sister looks like—and I think the girl on the video is her," stated one user, who wished to remain anonymous.

"The videos are just too much for my kiddos to handle," said Dhonielle Lee, a mother of four. "They watched one of the videos, and they had nightmares for months! Some of them look incredibly real. It gives me the creeps."

Sabrina skimmed the rest, which was basically just more of the same: anonymous sources who claimed to have "proof" that the videos were showing actual crimes, and parents complaining that the videos were too scary for their kids. After reading the article, Sabrina did a quick search to see if there was anything debunking the story on her favorite fact-checking websites, but she came up empty.

Interesting.

Evelyn had included a link to the Scream Site website, and Sabrina went back to her email and clicked it. She decided she may as well go straight to the source to see for herself.

A woman's high-pitched scream filled the air. Sabrina jumped, her heart pounding as she punched buttons to turn the volume down on her laptop. The screen went black, and large, bloodred letters slowly filled the screen:

ARE YOU READY TO SCREAM?

"Not really," Sabrina muttered, irritated that the silly trick had caught her off guard. She reminded herself not to be a gullible kid. She was in high school, after all. Almost an adult. Even if she didn't feel like it right now, sitting in the living room, checking the corners for imaginary monsters.

The red letters faded and a welcome screen appeared. "Click here to verify you are over thirteen," the box read. Sabrina clicked it, even though she always thought those verification tests were silly. That wasn't going to stop any kid she knew from clicking anyway to see something cool.

Once she'd clicked the box, the screen prompted her to log in or sign up for a new account. Sabrina quickly signed up, using the name Lizard2003. It was her go-to username, her favorite animal and the year her parents had bought their house in Port Riverton. Things no one would ever guess. When her dad had been alive, he'd drilled a respect for the Internet into both Sabrina and Faith, telling them often, "You can't just put anything you want on the Internet. The Internet is forever, and the stuff you post out there is like putting up a sign on a street corner. Anyone could see it, and anyone could use that information to hurt you or your family. So be smart and be responsible, because you can't undo anything you put there." It was a lecture that Sabrina never forgot.

Once she'd finished setting up her account, she logged in. The website was pretty straightforward. It looked like just about every other video site out there. A banner across the top of the screen displayed the most popular videos to date, with a list of most popular users running down the right-hand side. A flashing box in the middle of the screen prompted her to "Post your own terrifying tale!" A flashing red number one urged her to click on an envelope icon toward the top of the screen.

Sabrina paused for just a moment, then clicked on it and found a welcome message from the site administrator that explained the basics: Users were invited to post videos and join in the chats about the videos. Upvoted videos were featured on the landing page, and the user with the most upvoted videos by the end of the year would win a trip to Hollywood. It was just as Evelyn had said, only it didn't look like anything special to Sabrina. Where was the story here?

Sabrina clicked around a bit more, eventually settling on the top video of the day. It was posted by a user, MariannDawn1, who had almost five thousand followers.

"Wow, that's a lot of people," Sabrina murmured. It was strange she hadn't heard of Scream Site before this. With this many users, it was obviously pretty popular. How could she be this out of touch with what was trending? Maybe Evelyn was right. Maybe Sabrina was working too hard, not having enough fun. Maybe she was just that uncool and completely out of it.

Sabrina shrugged away the thought, clicked on the most popular video, and waited for it to play.

CHAPTER THREE

Sabrina had made a terrible mistake.

As the video began to play, she immediately wanted to stop it. What was she doing? She hated scary movies. So much. Horror movies were more Faith's speed. Sabrina liked to watch romantic comedies or documentaries. She liked puppies and animals and nature and meet-cutes, not serial killers and psychopaths. What was she doing on Scream Site?

But the video was already playing and Sabrina was too frozen to make it stop.

The images on the screen bounced as if someone was running. It was dark with only flashes of light from the camera, just enough to catch glimpses of trees, bits of blue clothing, and running shoes pounding through the leaves. Sabrina realized the girl wasn't just recording the video. She was also using the phone as a flashlight to guide her steps. Sabrina couldn't hear much, so she clicked up the volume. The sound of leaves crunching with each step and the girl gasping for air came crackling through the speakers. And then whispers through her ragged breath: "Please help me. This is real. This is real!"

And suddenly, a blood-curdling scream.

Sabrina's hands flew to cover her eyes by instinct. She could hear a man's voice singing some nursery rhyme in an eerily calm voice. Sabrina opened her eyes again in time to see the girl tripping and falling into a pile of leaves, then the heels of her sneakers digging into the dirt as she tried to scoot away. "Who are you? *What* are you?" she cried desperately. The camera fell to the ground, revealing a shot of the girl's face for the first time, ever so briefly.

The light caught on something shiny for just a moment before one final scream: "NO!"

The video stopped. The screen went black.

"Whoa," Sabrina said, her own pulse racing and icy beads of sweat clinging to her brow. She stared at the black screen for several seconds, processing what she'd just seen before slowly reaching out to her keyboard to push replay. She didn't want to ever see or hear those things again. Yet, she had to. She had to find something revealing that it was all fake. Like it was supposed to be. Background noise, a laugh, anything that would give it away. She found herself holding her breath as it played again. And again.

But there was nothing. The video looked real. And if it wasn't real, it was amazing acting.

Sabrina got to her feet and began to pace. It all looked and sounded believable, and nothing felt fake or staged. But was this what users of the site did—pull out all the stops just to get likes and try to win the competition? Sabrina couldn't help but come back to the same thought: If it was real, someone needed to help that girl.

The front door opened and slammed. Sabrina jumped and spun around to find her sister in the foyer. "Hey, what's wrong with you?" Faith asked.

"Me? Nothing. Why would you think something was wrong?"

Faith laughed, the sound so surprising to Sabrina that she relaxed a bit. She hadn't heard her sister laugh in what felt like forever.

"Your face is all flushed, and you look like you just ran up and down the stairs a bunch of times. What's going on? What're you looking at?" Faith asked, a sly tone in her voice.

"Scream Site," Sabrina admitted, turning the laptop around so that Faith could see the screen.

Faith's eyebrows shot up. "So, *you're* into horror sites, now?"

Sabrina shook her head so hard that her ponytail started to come loose. She put down her laptop and adjusted it. "Nope, not even a little. I've watched exactly one video."

Faith nodded. "And you got all freaked out over it?" She walked toward the couch and leaned over to see the laptop screen. "Which one was it . . . oh yeah, that's a good one," Faith said as she peered at the screen.

"You've seen it?"

"Yeah, I've watched most of the videos on there. Some of them are really good. Others . . . " Faith trailed off and shrugged. "Either way, I'm surprised you're watching them. Remember when we went to see *Your Blood Is Mine* and you and Mom had to leave halfway through the movie?" Faith grinned, and a hot flash of embarrassment welled up in Sabrina.

"Since that was just like a month ago, I do," Sabrina said, closing the laptop as she got her emotions under control. "I'm only on Scream Site because I have to find something to write about for the *Daily Sun* application, and I'm thinking this might be it. Did you know that there's a rumor that girls have gone missing after posting videos?"

Faith nodded. "Oh yeah, there are lots of rumors about the site." She began to tick them off on her fingers, "Girls have gone missing after posting or even just watching the videos; some of the videos are footage of actual crimes; the website was founded by a serial killer looking for victims; et cetera. You can see most of the theories on the message boards. There's a whole list of them. It's all just PR to drive traffic to the site, I'm guessing."

"Hmmm, I'll check them out later. I have a paper I have to write first, though." Sabrina picked up her laptop and started to head to her room.

Faith stopped her before she reached the stairs. "Wait, you don't think any of those are true, do you?"

Sabrina shrugged. She considered her next words carefully, not wanting to sound like a little kid but like a mature fourteen-year-old who had everything under control. "I don't know, maybe? There's usually some grain of truth in most rumors. Mrs. Wembley says that as journalists our job is to separate truth from opinion. So maybe there's some truth here to what people are talking about. Maybe girls aren't disappearing because of the website, but maybe there's something there." When Sabrina saw her sister's doubtful face, she decided to backpedal a bit. "At the very least, it seems that filming these fake movies could be dangerous. That could still be a pretty good story."

Faith laughed again and shook her head, like that was the funniest thing she'd ever heard. "OK, *Detective*. Well, I'm going to grab something to eat and then I'm heading over to Stephanie's house to study. I'll see you later."

"Later," Sabrina murmured as her sister walked into the kitchen. She slowly trudged up the stairs to her room, wondering what she should've said to Faith instead of what she had really been thinking. Because she didn't feel like a cool, smart, sophisticated teenager who could be working as an actual journalist someday soon.

She felt like the dumbest little sister in the world.

CHAPTER FOUR

Scream Site was all that Sabrina could think about the next day at school. It had taken her all night to finish her paper. By the time she had a chance to go back to look at the Scream Site message boards and make a list of the different conspiracies, she was bone tired, and she decided to go to bed instead.

But after she fell asleep, her dreams were plagued with visions of being chased through the woods by a shadowy figure. Every time she screamed for help, no one came. She was all alone, in the woods, with a crazed madman who was just about to strike—

That was when her alarm rang, startling her

awake. Sabrina had dragged herself into the shower, but she'd dozed off during homeroom and spent lunch yawning so widely that Evelyn finally said, "Maybe you should get a soda or something. There's no way you're going to make it through history class like that."

They were sitting at their favorite table in the cafeteria, the one close to the doors but far enough away from the trash cans that it didn't stink. Evelyn was eating her daily usual, pepperoni pizza, while Sabrina had a cheese sandwich she'd brought from home. It wasn't until Sabrina went to take a bite that she realized she had been so tired that she'd forgotten the cheese when she packed her lunch that morning.

Sabrina threw her bread "sandwich" back into her lunch bag and pulled out a banana. "Ugh, you're probably right. I'm supposed to meet Mrs. Wembley after school too, so it's not even like I'll be able to sneak home and take a nap," Sabrina said, yawning again.

"I thought you were going straight home to work on your paper last night? Did you get caught up in *Gem War Attack* or something?" Evelyn asked.

Gem War Attack was Sabrina's favorite show, and the distraction of a *Gem War Attack* marathon had been responsible for more than one late night homework session. But not this time. Sabrina shook her head. "No, I was busy looking at Scream Site. Well, only one video, really. But it freaked me out so much that I didn't sleep at all. I'm hoping that the same thing doesn't happen tonight. Otherwise I'll never be able to write this story."

Evelyn set down her pizza and leaned forward with a grin. "So, you *are* going to write about Scream Site?"

Sabrina nodded. "I think so. Faith said that there are lots of different theories in the message boards about the website, so I'm going to approach it more from the angle of trying to figure out what's real and what's fake. You know, like that lecture Mr. Nguyen gave us on fact versus fiction in the Internet age."

Evelyn groaned and sat back in her chair, all the excitement disappearing from her face. "I cannot believe you have actually managed to make something cool like an urban legend sound so, I don't know . . . *educational*."

Sabrina sat up straight and scowled at Evelyn. "This article is all that stands between me and a winning internship application, Ev. It has to be perfect, and that means it can't just be fun, it has to have some substance behind it."

"I suppose," Evelyn said. The bell rang, interrupting their conversation. "So, I guess this means no Lou's Brews after school?"

"Nah, sorry. But if you want to come over later, I

can order pizza and we can look at the website together. Tonight is my mom's late night at the hospital, so she won't be home for dinner." Sabrina didn't mention that she didn't exactly want to be home by herself while she was looking at Scream Site. It would make her sound like a child.

Evelyn grinned. "Free pizza? You know I'm there." There were few things Evelyn liked more than pizza.

"Great," Sabrina said. "It's a party."

She tried not to think about the fact that she was going to have to look at Scream Site a lot if she was actually going to write an article about it. Sometimes journalism was all about facing your fears.

* * *

A few hours later at her one-on-one meeting with Mrs. Wembley, the freshman English teacher and school newspaper advisor, Sabrina tried to explain her idea for a news feature. It wasn't going well. They were standing in the library computer lab, which was also the room most of the after-school clubs used. Today it was empty, since the Chess Club and Coding Club were both at tournaments and the Journalism Club only met on Tuesdays. Mrs. Wembley liked to host her meetings in the library so the students could use the computers to write and "follow their journalistic instincts" while considering research topics.

Today Sabrina felt like maybe her journalistic instincts had cut out after the final bell.

"OK, Sabrina, tell me about this website you're interested in writing about for your internship application. Scary Site?"

"Scream Site, Mrs. Wembley," Sabrina corrected, for what felt like the twentieth time.

Mrs. Wembley wasn't old, but she wasn't young either. Her short grayish-brown hair was cut in a no-nonsense pixie, and her skin was always tan from the long-distance running she did, even during the winter. But she also had a worn-out look to her, like something had made her very tired once and she'd never recovered. Sabrina thought maybe she'd been pretty long ago, but now she just looked exhausted, in sort of the same way Sabrina's mom had right after her dad had died. Maybe Mrs. Wembley had some sadness in her life too?

It was also Mrs. Wembley's distrust of technology that made her seem kind of old. Where Mrs. Sebastian liked hearing about the websites and tech tools her daughters were using, Mrs. Wembley usually pursed her lips in suspicion when her students mentioned things they'd seen on the Internet. She believed that books and "primary sources" were much more reliable ways to get information.

Sabrina tried again. "Scream Site has several

stories surrounding it—people saying that what's happening on the site might be happening in real life," Sabrina explained. She dug into her backpack and pulled out some of the screenshots she'd taken during her study period. Sometimes it was better to use printed pictures when things became unclear, and the shots of the website could better explain things to Mrs. Wembley than fuzzy-headed, sleep deprived Sabrina could. Especially since Mrs. Wembley read an actual newspaper every morning instead of reading the *Daily Sun* online.

While her teacher studied the printouts of the website, Sabrina kept talking. "The point of the site is to find new talent for a couple of well-known horror directors, the Scarapelli Brothers. But there have been rumors that the website is responsible for something sketchy. There are reports that girls may have gone missing after using the website, and it sounds like police have had to investigate things in connection with the site." That last part was a bit of a stretch, but Sabrina *assumed* that police had looked into it. She could worry about making the pieces fit in her story once she'd done a little more research.

"The police?" Mrs. Wembley said, with some degree of alarm. "Sabrina, I don't want you out there investigating things that are actually dangerous. This is a school newspaper, not the *New York Times*, for heaven's sake. We don't exactly have the expertise to investigate real crimes. Not to mention that it would be highly inappropriate for me to send a student after a story that had the potential to be unsafe."

"It's not dangerous," Sabrina said, quickly redirecting. "It's less about what is actually happening on the website and more about what people *think* is happening. The idea of perception and how to tell truth from fiction. Scream Site is just the backdrop to that."

"So," Mrs. Wembley said, scratching her head with her pencil, "you want to write about people believing these videos are real. But that might just fan the flames of the misperception, so to speak. It could give some validity to all the hearsay." She shook her head. "A story about the dangers of the Internet would be more worthwhile, and targeted to a broader audience. You could talk about the possibility of identity theft, the security of information, the possibility of doxing—where someone posts your private information on a website. These are issues that people should really be informed about."

Sabrina knew it was Mrs. Wembley's job as the journalism adviser to make her think about the angle on a story before she went after it, but for some reason today Sabrina felt a little defensive. She had to ask herself, why *did* she want to investigate Scream Site?

She didn't even like scary videos or movies, and last night had proven that they definitely didn't like her. Researching anything about the website was sure to make for more sleepless nights.

Maybe Mrs. Wembley was right. Maybe this was just a fluff piece, a cool story to share with friends and not the real journalism that Sabrina was looking for. Maybe she should take the safety angle Mrs. Wembley was suggesting. Either that or find something else to write about all together.

But then Sabrina thought back to the girl begging for help, and the quaver in her voice. Sabrina was pretty good at telling a truth from a lie. She spent a lot of time on those debunking websites, so she felt like she had the skills to spot fake content, and this video had felt real in a way that was hard to describe. She felt deep down in the soul of her being that something about that video was truly dangerous.

And that meant there was a story there to be investigated.

"Mrs. Wembley," Sabrina began again, standing straighter and looking her teacher in the eye. "I can definitely work something about Internet safety into the piece, but that isn't the big story here. The video I saw last night? Well, I don't believe it was fake. And a lot of other people don't think some of the other videos are fake, either. So I think it's worthwhile to question that. Why do the videos feel so real, and how does the line between reality and pretend begin to blur? And if there's any kind of truth behind the videos, anything sketchy at all, I'll turn that information over to the police. It's not like I would get personally involved. . . . "

Mrs. Wembley still didn't look convinced, so Sabrina kept talking. "It's what I want to write about for my application. If you don't think it's right for the school paper article, then I could write about graduation for that instead. But I think there's something here, some deeper story that needs to get out to the world. If I'm wrong, I'm wrong. But if I'm right, then there's a girl out there who may have been hurt, and no one seems to care and no one is looking for her. Didn't you say that a journalist has a responsibility to shed light into the dark corners of society? I think this is a dark corner I should check out."

Mrs. Wembley leaned back in her chair, a slight smile playing around her lips. "Well, all right then. First draft for the school paper is in two weeks. That should also give you time to get it ready for the *Daily Sun* internship."

Sabrina smiled, and her fatigue slipped away. "Thanks, Mrs. Wembley," she said.

"Oh, and Sabrina," Mrs. Wembley called. Sabrina paused in the doorway.

"Be careful. If something nefarious really is happening behind the scenes, you wouldn't want to get caught up in it."

Sabrina nodded and headed out the door, a hop in her step.

She had a story to investigate. That internship just might be within her grasp.

CHAPTER FIVE

Once she got home, Sabrina knocked out her algebra and English homework in record time. She was just sitting down to start researching Scream Site when the doorbell rang and Evelyn walked in with two pizzas from Sorrento's, the local pizza place.

"I wanted to make sure you didn't stick me with pineapple again," she said, setting the boxes down on the coffee table in the living room.

"Pineapple pizza is delicious," Sabrina objected, opening the boxes and peeking in. Pizza scented steam wafted out. Inside the first box was a mushroom and pepperoni pizza. That was Evelyn's. The second contained pineapple and jalapenos, Sabrina's favorite. Sabrina smiled, glad that her friend knew her so well.

"Can we eat before we get into these website shenanigans?" Evelyn asked. "I have to tell you what happened at the store today." She went to the kitchen and came back with two plates and a couple of cans of soda. Evelyn was at Sabrina's house so often that she sometimes behaved like she lived there, an observation Faith had snarkily made on more than one occasion.

"OK, but I need you to stick around when I start researching Scream Site. I don't want to freak myself out again like I did last night," Sabrina said.

Evelyn laughed. "You are such a weenie."

"It was seriously bad, Ev. I was sitting in the living room with all the lights on waiting for some slasher guy to come after me."

The girls ate pizza until there was nothing left but a few forlorn crusts. While they ate, Evelyn told Sabrina about the guy who'd come to the store looking for a very strange Chinese powder because he was collecting ingredients for a spell, even though Chao's store didn't sell Chinese herbal remedies and was mostly focused on fresh produce and quality meats. "I swear, people see 'Chao's Grocery' and can only imagine it to be one thing. It's super rude and kind of racist."

"People are the worst," Sabrina agreed.

Evelyn leaned back and groaned, her straight dark hair falling across her face, its new purple stripe gleaming brightly. "I am so full of pizza I feel like my belly is going to explode."

"Great, it's a perfect time to research, then!" Sabrina said, clearing the plates and the pizza boxes. Evelyn kept groaning about her full belly while Sabrina cleaned up the rest of the mess and brought out her laptop.

Evelyn pulled herself out of the chair she'd landed in and sat down next to Sabrina. "OK, so what's the deal? What are you doing, watching videos?"

Sabrina pulled up Scream Site, logged in, and clicked through the welcome screen to get to her personal home page. "I want to figure out how I would look up any of the theories about Scream Site. Faith mentioned a message board, but there's so much to click on here that I keep getting lost."

"Oh, the message boards? Here . . . " Evelyn took the laptop and showed Sabrina how to get there with a few clicks. "Most of the stuff on the message boards is just people asking for folks to upvote their videos or whatever, but there's one thread that's pretty good. See this here? It's a search function and you can type in a few keywords . . . ah! Here it is."

Evelyn handed Sabrina back the laptop. She'd

clicked on a message with the title "Are People Disappearing After Using Scream Site?" It was exactly what Sabrina was looking for. She quickly scanned through the responses:

redrum1: So, I heard that there are several rumors on Scream Site about girls going missing, and people have even pointed to a few videos by users as proof. Thoughts?

girlonfilm23: it's all just people jealous that some posters are doing better than others. just rumors.

redrum1: It does mostly seem to get started every time someone has a video hit the top 10 landing page. Video of the day makes people say some crazy stuff. Haters gonna hate, yanno

torontosweetie: I think it's true. So far there's been three girls who've disappeared. It's weird. It creeps me out more than shady99's videos.

girlonfilm23: proof?

felixthecat89: right, where's the police investigation? you don't think the cops would shut this place down if there were girls disappearing?

There were a lot more responses of people asking for proof and dismissing the original poster's question, but then suddenly there was a single response that stopped Sabrina and sent a chill racing down her spine.

kittykat1000: I think this is true, but no one will believe me. My sister, MariannDawn1, used to post all the time and now she's missing. I need your help. 2 days ago my sister disappeared, and yesterday someone else posted on her account. I need to find my sister. Please if anyone has any news about MariannDawn1, please, please dm me.

redrum1: Are you serious?

kittykat1000: Yes. Please, if anyone has heard anything from her, please just let me know.

torontosweetie: Yeah, ok, whatever. Nice way to promo her videos.

kittykat1000: I'm not! A video was posted after my sister disappeared that wasn't one of hers. Please, I just want to find her. You don't have to watch the videos, just call the Port Riverton Police Department in Maryland. I swear, this isn't me trying to get clicks.

torontosweetie: Yeah, ok. Sure.

Sabrina pointed at the screen. "That's the name of the girl in the video I watched—Mariann Dawn! Oh wow. Ev, it looks like maybe the rumor is true. Girls really have gone missing after using Scream Site. Did you see this before?"

Evelyn shook her head. "I just knew about it because some guys in my French class were talking about it. But this just seems like typical Internet drama. You aren't really buying this, are you?"

Sabrina scanned through the messages once more and gnawed on her bottom lip. "I don't know. Why would someone jump on a message board and claim that their sister had gone missing?"

Evelyn threw her hands up. "For the same reason anyone does anything—attention! This girl is obviously using a rumor to promote her work. I mean, how do we even know that's her sister? It could be the same person with two user accounts, sending traffic to her MariannDawn1 account videos to get clicks." She shook her head. "Think about it, Sabrina. People lie on the Internet all the time."

Sabrina didn't respond but kept scrolling through the messages, eventually clicking on the one that asked anyone who knew anything to call the Port Riverton Police Department. "If this isn't real, why did she ask people to call the police—our local police department?" Sabrina asked.

Evelyn leaned forward and peered at the posting. "Well, yeah, that is weird. I mean, I still think it's fake, but it's a gutsy move to involve the cops in your scam. Maybe she just went all in."

Sabrina bit her lip. "Let's find out."

CHAPTER SIX

"We should reach out to her," Sabrina said, opening a messaging screen.

Evelyn snatched the laptop out of Sabrina's hands. "Who, kittykat1000? Are you insane?"

"Yes! You said it yourself, this person lives near us. Otherwise, why Port Riverton Police Department? Why not a big city like Boston or Baltimore?" Sabrina asked. She took the laptop back and tapped the screen. "And look, this post is only a week old. I should send her a direct message and see if she'll talk to me."

Evelyn widened her eyes and shook her head. "You have no idea who that person really is! What if she's actually like some forty-year-old dude who uses the message boards to stalk teenage girls? You'll be walking right into his trap."

"I don't think that weird older guys pretend their sister went missing to find new victims. Or ask people to contact the police department. But how about this: Let's investigate them and see if they've posted any videos. If they're from Port Riverton, we might know them, right?"

Evelyn sighed. "OK, fine. But no direct messages until we know who they are for sure. I swear, you're like a cautionary tale just waiting to happen."

Sabrina clicked on kittykat1000's profile. The profile picture was of a missing poster, and Sabrina clicked the image to enlarge it.

"Hey, I know that poster," Evelyn said after it filled the screen. "The missing girl is Mariann Sanchez. She graduated with my brother. A woman who looked like she was about twenty came by the store and asked to hang that poster in the front window. She said her sister Mariann went missing and she was hoping maybe the poster would get someone to talk. We still have it up."

"So the person who came into your store must have been kittykat1000," Sabrina said.

Evelyn shrugged. "I guess. But it's weird we didn't hear anything about this. I mean, they practically do school announcements every time someone loses change in a vending machine. You would think everyone would have made a big deal out of some teen girl going missing. Like, it would be on the news, wouldn't it?"

Sabrina frowned. Evelyn was right, and it was a good question. If Mariann Sanchez had been kidnapped, where were the search parties and police action and all the stuff that usually happened when someone was lost?

The poster on the screen wasn't anything special. The top said MISSING in all capital letters and noted she'd last been seen April fourth. Right below the headline was a picture of a pretty Latina girl, Mariann Sanchez. It was obviously a selfie, and she appeared happy in the picture.

Sabrina did an Internet search for her name, and a couple of local news articles came up. "It looks like her sister did report her missing, but her friends and the aunt who raised the girls said that they believed she'd run off to Hollywood to become an actress. She's over eighteen, so not a minor anymore. But her aunt thought Mariann was wasting time with her acting."

"Well, I guess that explains why we didn't hear anything," Evelyn said.

"But her sister still seems to think that she's gone missing for real," Sabrina said.

"Right, but that's not surprising. I don't know everything my brother does. Do you know everything Faith does?" Evelyn asked.

Sabrina shook her head. "No, not anymore." She bit her lip and kept clicking through a bunch of pictures of Mariann Sanchez from different social media sites. Sabrina stared at the girl for a long moment. She was happy and smiling in all these photos. Nothing like the girl screaming for help in the video that Sabrina had watched the day before. But they were the same person.

"Evelyn, you've got to watch that video," Sabrina said. She navigated to the video that had been uploaded to MariannDawn1's account.

"Oh. Wow," Evelyn said as she watched, the color draining from her face. "That . . . doesn't look fake."

"No, it doesn't," Sabrina said, relieved that someone agreed with her, but disturbed all over again as she watched Mariann call for help that never came. A girl who was now supposedly missing, and whose sister was begging for help on message boards.

Sabrina always followed her instincts when it came to a story, and this was no different. Her gut was telling her that the girl in the video really was in trouble, and that kittykat1000 might know more about Scream Site and whatever was happening there than anyone else.

Sabrina had enabled auto play last night after clicking on the video again and again, so now it replayed on an endless loop. The girls watched it, mesmerized, each time with the same inevitable ending.

"I'm going to message kittykat," Sabrina said again, snapping out of her trance.

"This is super creepy," Evelyn conceded, but she stopped Sabrina before she could take the laptop back. "But here's a question: If someone is taking girls, how did this video get posted after she went missing? If she's been kidnapped, there's no way she would have been able to post this to her own account."

Sabrina gnawed on her bottom lip as she thought. "I don't know. The simplest explanation is that the person who took her got access to her account and uploaded it. Maybe, like, as a warning?"

"I don't know," Evelyn said. "It seems to me that it's more likely that she posted the video herself. Maybe she really did run away, and her sister just doesn't want to admit it?"

The video had reached its terrifying conclusion and was about to play yet again, but Sabrina stopped it. She clicked to the messaging page.

"Maybe they made her tell them her password and stuff," Sabrina said while she began to type an instant message to kittykat1000.

"I think it's way more likely that she's alive and well in Hollywood, trying to get her career off the ground," Evelyn said. "It's sad that she left her sister in the dark, but I bet that's why the police and the media haven't made a big deal about her disappearance. The sister is probably just in denial that Mariann didn't tell her she was leaving."

"It's possible . . . ," Sabrina said, even though she didn't believe that. Just thinking about what really might have happened to Mariann made her break into a cold sweat. "But I still want to talk to this kittykat person."

Sabrina took a breath and then hit the send button on her message. "There, it's sent."

"What did you say?" Evelyn asked.

"I told her that I live in Port Riverton and that I'm working on a story about the possibility of disappearances that could be linked to Scream Site. And that—"

There was a dinging noise, and Sabrina jumped in surprise. "Wow, that was fast."

"She replied already?"

Sabrina nodded. "She says she would be grateful for the chance to talk to me and wants to meet at Lou's Brews tomorrow at four p.m."

Evelyn's eyes widened in surprise. "Well, I guess you'd better come up with some questions to ask.

And we also need to figure out a plan."

Sabrina frowned. "A plan? What for?"

"Just in case kittykat1000 is actually the person who kidnapped MariannDawn1."

CHAPTER
SEVEN

The next day at school, all Sabrina could think about was her meeting with kittykat1000. She still didn't know the user's real name, and she was a bit worried about that. But she also figured that Lou's Brews was the perfect place to meet a complete stranger. It was totally public, and lots of people would be around. Besides, it wasn't like she'd given out her phone number and address.

Still, her dad's warning words niggled at her conscience. Meeting up with strangers was reckless and completely unlike Sabrina. But she needed to hear what Mariann's sister had to say. Was she just a girl in denial about her sister running off to Hollywood, as Evelyn thought, or was there really something going on? Something dark and nefarious, as Mrs. Wembley had warned her against?

Sabrina knew it was a bad idea to meet up with Internet randos, so she hadn't worn the yellow shirt she'd told kittykat1000 she'd be wearing. Instead, she wore a red shirt with a black cat pattern on it. Now, without revealing herself, she could surreptitiously scan for kittykat1000, who said she'd be carrying a motorcycle helmet and wearing a jean jacket. Sabrina could discretely slip away in case kittykat turned out to be someone she didn't want to meet.

But when Sabrina got to Lou's Brews at four o'clock on the dot, the woman she found sitting at a table wearing a jean jacket and cradling a motorcycle helmet in her arms was just a normal person. She looked about twenty, as Evelyn had said, and she had an expression that was equal parts tired and sad. Her long dark hair was pulled into a high ponytail and her skin was a few shades lighter that Sabrina's. As Sabrina got closer, she noticed that the woman's eyes were red rimmed, and her nose was pink as well, as though she'd been crying.

"Are you kittykat1000?" Sabrina asked tentatively.

The woman startled as she looked up. "I'm sorry, do I know you?"

"I'm Lizard2003. On Scream Site. My real name is Sabrina. I sent you a message about your missing sister?"

"Wait, are you serious? You're just a kid," she said, her voice filled with disgust. She stood to go. "Look, I don't have time for jokes."

"Wait, it's not a joke! I'm writing a story about the rumor that girls have gone missing after using Scream Site. Well, actually so far there's just your sister, but part of my research is to figure out if there might be others too. I watched the video she posted. It looked real. I don't care what anyone says."

"Well, that's great, but what are you going to do that the police can't? I already talked to them, and they're convinced that my sister just took off."

After scheduling to meet with kittykat1000, Sabrina had spent the evening searching for more articles about Mariann's disappearance. Most of them seemed to agree that she had run away. "Do you think that's true? That maybe she could have run off?" Sabrina asked.

"Of course it isn't true!" the woman said, her voice rising slightly. A few people in the café turned to stare at them, and she closed her eyes for a long moment before continuing. "My sister wouldn't do that. She isn't like that. She's just finishing her first year of community college and she wants to be a film director.

Everyone keeps saying that she's just another flighty actress wannabe. She may be flighty, but it's not like her to just up and run away. I would've known if she was planning something. But the police don't seem to care about anything I tell them. And if they can't help me, I'm pretty sure a scrawny kid can't."

"I'm not a kid, and I can help you." Sabrina's brain searched for a way to earn this woman's trust. If she left, there went her one good lead. "Wait, you spoke with the police. Who did you speak with?"

"Detective Francis."

Sabrina smiled in relief. "John Francis?"

The girl crossed her arms. "Yeah, why? You know him?"

"He's my uncle. My mom's brother. So I know him pretty well. Plus, my dad used to be a cop. . . . So, there might be something you can tell me that would help his investigation. And if I did bring him any information, I know he'd listen to me."

That last part wasn't entirely true. Detective Francis was Sabrina's uncle, and he was always willing to help the Sebastian family around the house since her dad was no longer there, but it wasn't like they ever discussed his casework.

Of course, it wasn't like she'd ever asked, either.

Sabrina held her breath and waited for Mariann's sister to make her decision. She was the only lead

Sabrina had on this story, and if she walked out that door, Sabrina would be back to square one. She hoped her speech had been convincing enough to make this woman consider trusting her.

A pang of guilt twinged through Sabrina. Was that the only reason she cared about Mariann—the fact that she might be part of a juicy news story? No. Sabrina did want to help, if she could. The woman staring at Sabrina was obviously heartbroken. How would Sabrina feel if it was Faith who had gone missing? If the police dismissed Faith's absence because they assumed she had just run off?

Sabrina would be heartbroken as well.

The woman watched Sabrina for a long moment before sighing and sitting back down at the table. "OK, fine. What do you want to know? You've got ten minutes."

Sabrina nodded, pulled out her phone, and got ready to work. She might be about to get the scoop of her life.

CHAPTER EIGHT

Sabrina opened the recording app on her phone. "Do you mind if I record this?"

"Nope, go ahead." The woman crossed her arms and leaned back in the chair across from Sabrina, stretching out her long legs. She was trying to look relaxed, but Sabrina could still see worry in her eyes. And more than a little annoyance. She clearly thought her time was being wasted, and that made Sabrina tense—and even more determined to be as professional as a real reporter.

Sabrina tapped record on the app. "Please tell me your name."

"My name is Lupe Sanchez. I'm kittykat1000 on Scream Site."

"And your sister?"

"Her name is Mariann Sanchez—MariannDawn1 on Scream Site."

Sabrina pulled out her list of questions, her hands starting to shake a bit. This was her first real deal interview, and she really didn't want to mess it up. "OK, so your sister went missing April fourth."

Lupe sniffed and nodded. "The day after her birthday. She was supposed to go and hang out with some guy she'd met through Scream Site at Funland."

Sabrina wrinkled her brow. "The amusement park?" She had memories of going there years ago with their dad. He'd pretend to cheat at mini-golf and then laugh when Faith and Sabrina caught him. And he'd let the girls pig out on hot dogs and cotton candy. Mrs. Sebastian always assumed the stomachaches they had when they got home were motion sickness from the Ferris wheel.

Lupe nodded, and the wistful expression on her face dragged Sabrina back to the present. "Yeah, Mariann loved the go-karts. The park is closed now, but my sister and her friends were always shooting videos out there because it's pretty much abandoned. This guy she knew wanted to shoot a video in the woods right next to the park."

"Why did the park close?" Sabrina thought it was weird that she hadn't heard anything about it shutting down. Usually news like that was a big deal, especially since there wasn't much to do in Port Riverton.

Lupe shrugged. "I don't know. They closed down for the season last fall, like they usually do. But from what I heard, something terrible happened to the owner, and the park has gone out of business because of it."

Sabrina nodded and made a note to find out more about Funland closing. Then she turned her attention back to Lupe. "Are those the Funland woods seen in the final video posted to Scream Site under Mariann's account?"

Lupe shrugged again, her expression guarded. "I don't know, maybe? Anyway, she didn't come home that night, and when she still wasn't back the next day, I called the police."

"Did she leave a note or anything?" Sabrina asked. It sounded like something a reporter would ask.

"Nothing. We're roommates. She's only a year younger than me, but I'm still the older sister. I'm supposed to take care of her. I should've been there to protect her. She always said I was overprotective, but I was just doing what I had to do," Lupe said, reaching up to wipe a tear from her eye.

Sabrina nodded and wrote down the details.

"So, who was the guy she had been talking to on the website?"

"No clue. Mariann said he went by the handle Asher3245, but when I logged in to try to message him after she went missing, his account was gone."

Sabrina frowned. "Wait, so you saw the Asher3245 account before she went missing?"

"Yes. She even sent me a few pictures of him, because I told her there's nothing but creepers on the Internet and you never know who you're talking to. Here, let me see if I still have it." Lupe picked up her phone and scrolled through the pictures. "I gave it to the police, but they said they talked to the guy and he claimed to have nothing to do with her disappearance."

Lupe held up her phone so Sabrina could see the picture of Mariann's mystery boy. Sabrina frowned. "I know him. He goes to my school. Asher Grey. He's in my sister's grade."

"Yeah, well, the police talked to him and he swears he doesn't know anything. He told them he never talked to her online and said that someone must have hacked his account. As far as I know, that's all the police have done. They keep telling me there aren't any leads, that she ran away, and hopefully she'll come home on her own when her plans fall through. But I think they just don't care," Lupe said, her voice hardening as she talked about the police.

Sabrina swallowed down her agitation. She knew that police officers were overworked, especially in a town like Port Riverton, where there were only a few officers handling everything from traffic stops to violent crimes. She didn't like people to speak badly about them. Still, maybe there was something weird going on here. It didn't sound like Sabrina's Uncle John to just write off a case about a missing girl, but Sabrina didn't really know anything about police work. Maybe there was more happening in the investigation than Lupe knew?

"Did Mariann have any enemies?" Sabrina asked, taking notes quickly now as her brain began to work through the angles of the story.

"Not in real life. There were a few people on Scream Site who were mad when she was the number one video of the day a little while back. There's a pretty big prize for winning the competition, and people are super competitive. But other than that? I don't think so."

"So, no one who would maybe want to hurt her?"

Lupe's face grew stormy, and she shook her head. "No, everyone liked my sister. Well, except for Shady99. Some of the messages they sent were . . . weird."

"Weird how? Like threats?" Sabrina asked. She

remembered seeing that name on the message board.

"Yeah. It was almost like they knew Mariann. They knew things about her that only someone who had met her would know. It was creepy, like they'd hacked her computer or something. They knew where she went to school, the place where she worked, lots of stuff. She was freaked out at first, but then the messages stopped, and she figured they'd moved on to other things. I thought it was maybe this jealous girl she'd known in high school or someone like that. You know how the Internet is, no one is ever who they say they are."

Sabrina didn't know, because other than a few fanfiction websites, she didn't really interact much with people on social media. When Mr. Sebastian was still alive, he hadn't liked his daughters using any social media, and after he died, it had seemed almost disrespectful to his memory to open up new accounts. So mostly she just texted back and forth with Evelyn and read news articles.

But Sabrina didn't admit that to Lupe. She just said, "Oh, right, definitely."

Lupe sighed. "Listen, I have to get going. If it would help, I'll give you her login information so you can see all her activity on the site yourself. I gave it to the police, but they seemed kind of uninterested in it. Maybe you can find some clues in it."

Sabrina nodded. "That would be great, thanks. I'll do anything I can to help." She slid her notebook across the table and Lupe scribbled some stuff in it.

Lupe stood to go. "I know you're just a kid, and I know you probably aren't going to find anything the police haven't, but be careful, OK? Mariann is kind of a free spirit, but she's not careless. If someone got to her, if someone hurt her, well, I just don't want to see a poster around town with your face on it next."

Lupe picked up her motorcycle helmet and walked out of the café, leaving Sabrina with a whole bunch of questions and zero answers.

CHAPTER NINE

After Lupe left, Sabrina grabbed a sandwich from Lou's—turkey on rye with vinegar coleslaw and Swiss cheese—then hopped on her bike and pedaled home. The day was warm, like spring had finally kicked winter to the curb. Any day now the trees would be blooming in a riot of color, and Evelyn would be complaining about her allergies and that Mother Nature was a jerk.

Once she was at home, Sabrina put her sandwich in the fridge and called Evelyn.

"Nice to hear you weren't kidnapped," Evelyn said as she picked up.

"Not funny, Ev. Mariann is for real missing." Sabrina quickly filled Evelyn in on her conversation with Lupe. "I really think there's something bad going on here. I don't know what, but I'm going to out."

"So, you have a plan, now?"

"I do," Sabrina said. "Lupe said Mariann and her friends shot a lot of their videos in and around Funland. Did you know the park closed?"

"Really?" Evelyn said, surprise in her voice. "We just went there last summer."

"Yeah, because you had a crush on some guy who worked the mini-golf booth," Sabrina said.

"Um, that was not just 'some guy,' working the mini-golf booth—it was the one and only Asher Grey."

Sabrina paused. "Really? I thought his name was Aaron something."

"Nope," Evelyn said, the word loud and final. "It was Asher Grey. He just had a buzz cut instead of the floppy hair he has now. Trust me, I would know Asher anywhere."

Sabrina frowned. This was the second time today she'd heard Asher's name. She filed the information away for later and returned to the conversation. "Anyway, Lupe said the owner had trouble of some sort, and now Funland is closed. I think maybe that video Mariann posted was filmed in the woods right next to the park. We should check it out tomorrow after school if you have time."

"OK, let's be careful here, Scooby Doo. This creeper might already have one victim. We don't need to become the next ones."

Sabrina sighed. "I know. That's why I'm going to talk to my uncle. If there's something serious here, he can take care of it."

"Uncle? Oh, right. Detective Francis. Well, count me out of those field trips. Last time I saw him he threatened to give me a ticket for skateboarding in the no-skate zone at the park. My parents were so mad at me when he called them."

"You almost knocked that old lady over when you jumped the curb!" Sabrina said, remembering the day. It had been back in eighth grade. They'd gone to the park, mostly because there was a boy that Evelyn liked who skated there all the time. Evelyn wasn't shy about showing off in front of boys, especially cute ones.

"So, get this, since you are the expert on all things Asher," Sabrina continued. "Apparently Asher Grey was connected with Mariann somehow."

On the other end of the call, Evelyn made a choked sound. "Not possible, Sabrina. Everyone knows him—he's the hottest boy at school. And everyone knows when he's dating someone, because that means he's off the market, tragically. Even you would have heard that. Why the sudden interest in my future husband?"

Sabrina rolled her eyes, even though Evelyn couldn't see it. "I don't know that they were actually dating. But his picture was on a Scream Site message asking Mariann to meet him at Funland. So he's definitely on my list."

Evelyn laughed. "Are you serious, Sabrina? In addition to being the hottest guy, Asher is also like the nicest guy in the entire school. He volunteers at an animal shelter, like some sort of saint. His mom is a veterinarian, and he's always taking everyone's rescued cats and dogs to her for free check-ups. Asher Grey is not a psycho-kidnapper."

"We don't know that, Ev. I have to keep my options open. Cute guy or not. Anyway, I need to get my homework done so I can check out that Shady99 person. Lupe said they sent Mariann some threats."

"Well, be careful there, Detective. And let me know if you need any help, other than that stomping through the woods thing. I'm pretty good at underhanded dealings."

"Evelyn, we are not going to hack into anyone's user accounts. Besides, you are terrible at that sort of stuff. Remember the time you were convinced you could hack into Mr. Nguyen's teacher account and change your grade?" Sabrina said.

"If you would've let me keep trying, I definitely

would've gotten into the account. I didn't spend a whole summer at Hacker U for nothing." Evelyn's parents had made her take a coding class one summer, and ever since, she'd been dying to try to break into someone's account, even though it was super illegal. And she was pretty bad at it. That was just Evelyn: If you told her no, she was determined to make it a yes.

"We are not going to hack anything," Sabrina said again.

"Fine. You're no fun. Talk to you later."

"Bye." Sabrina ended the call and put her phone in her back pocket. She thought about Shady99. Could Shady99 and Asher3245 have anything to do with each other? The only way to figure it out would be to investigate. But not on an empty stomach.

She grabbed her sandwich and a soda from the fridge and headed upstairs to get to work.

CHAPTER TEN

Logging into Scream Site after talking to Lupe made Sabrina even more uneasy. Before, the only thing she'd really been worried about was whether she might see a scary video and get too freaked out to sleep the rest of the night. Now she knew that there might be something even more sinister about the site, and the idea of logging in gave her a feeling like walking into a graveyard—dark and foreboding.

Sabrina wanted to check out Mariann's account. But first, she decided she needed to get better acquainted with the site itself.

She hadn't really spent much time on the social part

of Scream Site. She'd been more focused on watching the videos—specifically Mariann's last video—than anything else. But Scream Site was more than just a video aggregator. Part of the site, in addition to the videos, message boards, and direct messaging system, was called Billboard. Sabrina discovered that people used their personal billboards to promote their own videos or to share other users' videos that they liked. Sabrina clicked on her own billboard. It was blank, of course, with a generic message that told visitors that she hadn't set it up yet.

Sabrina clicked in the search box at the top of the page and typed in MariannDawn1. The page loaded a copy of the missing poster that depicted a happy, smiling Mariann, with a note asking anyone who might have information to call.

So, if Mariann had run away and was still able to access her account, wouldn't she have taken down the poster? What kind of jerk would let people think she was missing if she was really just living a new life somewhere else? Sabrina supposed it was possible that Mariann had just abandoned her account, if she really had left town and moved on to other things. Maybe she hadn't seen it. Or, if she really was missing, she might not have access to her account anymore.

Another option occurred to Sabrina. Could Evelyn's theory be right, and Lupe and Mariann were in on some scam together? Had Lupe helped her sister create a fake kidnapping to generate interest in her videos? Lupe had said that Mariann wanted to be a director. What if this was all just some kind of ploy for attention?

Sabrina leaned back and considered the logistics of running such a scam. Could this all be a giant hoax? Would someone actually sink that low? And was Lupe in on it, or was she getting taken by her sister too?

Sabrina had seen how upset and emotionally wrecked Lupe was. She couldn't imagine that she was in on any sick publicity ploy on a silly website— unless she was the world's greatest actor. Maybe she had Hollywood aspirations of her own? But at the bottom of the poster was the number for the local police department. That seemed extremely risky for a marketing stunt. Wouldn't that be fraud or something?

Sabrina clicked on a few more of Mariann's videos, just to get an idea of what she'd been posting before her final video. Most of them were jump scares: videos of Mariann walking through a dark hallway or an alley and then someone jumping out at her, and at the viewer. They were filmed in a similar style to the video in the woods, but they lacked the authenticity of her last video. These clips felt fake. They looked like something a girl who had just graduated high school and had no film experience would make.

They were decent, but nothing compared to the video of Mariann being chased through the woods. So what had changed? An actual knife-wielding maniac chasing her?

Sabrina went back to the login screen, deleting her information and putting in the login for Mariann's account instead. She clicked through the messages, most of which were from people telling Mariann how much they loved her videos.

There were also a few messages from guys trying to flirt with Mariann. Sabrina rolled her eyes, clicking past those until she got to the ones from Asher3245.

Asher3245: Hey, I watched your video. Super cool, by the way. I don't know if you remember me from last year, but we had a class together. I was a sophomore when you were a senior.

MariannDawn1: o rly? what school?

Asher3245: Mount Clare. You had a purple backpack. We had wood shop together. You made a birdfeeder for your final project.

MariannDawn1: wait, is this who i think it is? pics or i block you.

The next message was the picture of Asher that Lupe had shown her. Sabrina recognized it from the food shelf drive the Key Club had done in the fall. It was a great picture of him, smiling with the sun glinting off his blond hair like he was in an ad for pimple cream or something. Evelyn was right, Asher was hot.

"I can see why you fell for it, Mariann. He is

cute—even though he's too young for you," Sabrina mumbled, taking a bite of her sandwich. She clicked through the rest of the messages. Asher3245 seemed to be asking a lot of questions about her filmmaking—where she got her ideas, where she shot her stuff, and who was helping her. At least they weren't the super flirty type of messages other users had posted to her.

Sabrina got to the last message, which was Asher3245 inviting Mariann to hang out at Funland on the Friday she disappeared. Sabrina closed out of the message chain and clicked on a different one. This one was from a couple of weeks before the chain with Asher3245. The messages were from user Shady99, and reading them gave Sabrina chills.

Shady99: The #1 spot is mine. Your videos are a cheap rip-off. Only I get to record at Funland. Delete your account or you're next.

MariannDawn1: lolol, whatever. your videos suck.

Shady99: I'M COMING FOR YOU.

That was all there was to the message string. Lupe had mentioned that Mariann had gotten a lot of harassing messages, but when Sabrina clicked through the different message chains, there wasn't anything else. Maybe Mariann had been freaked out enough to delete them. Or maybe there never were any other harassing messages?

How would it have felt to have someone know

enough about you to threaten you personally? If someone did take Mariann, they must have known her pretty well, to know where she'd gone to high school and what color her backpack was. It was eerie. Sabrina got up and turned her bedroom light on, rubbing her hands over her arms to try to chase away the chill of foreboding she suddenly felt. Reading through Mariann's messages by herself hadn't been the best idea. It made her imagination run overtime, thinking about what it was all heading toward.

But at least now she had a good lead. She'd talk to Asher tomorrow.

The lights in the house flickered—once, then twice.

And then the lights went out.

CHAPTER ELEVEN

Sabrina sat alone in the sudden dark, her computer screen the only illumination. Shady99's messages glared at her from the screen: "I'M COMING FOR YOU." For a single moment, she wondered if maybe somehow Shady99 had found *her* and was messing with her, playing with her electricity to freak her out?

Sabrina shook her head and pushed the silly thought aside. It was just the breaker going out as usual.

Sabrina fumbled around in the dark until she found her phone, to use the flashlight. The too-bright light threw her room into stark contrast of shadows and light, rendering her desk and bed into vague, monstrous shapes.

"We really need to fix that stupid breaker," Sabrina muttered, her heart pounding as she navigated through the dark.

She made her way downstairs carefully. She was almost to the bottom stair when she thought she heard a *creak*, like someone stepping on a loose floorboard in the house. Sabrina froze, her pulse pounding in her ears as she listened closely for another sound.

"Faith, is that you?" she called. Mrs. Sebastian wouldn't be home for another couple of hours, but Sabrina was sure she'd heard something. Hadn't she?

Was all this Scream Site nonsense just getting to her?

Sabrina hurried to the breaker box, holding her breath and trying to make as little noise as possible. Now that she'd convinced herself that someone else was in the house, she felt a million eyes watching her, and the same panic that she'd experienced the first time she'd watched Mariann's video. Sabrina didn't even try to calm her pounding heart and sweat-slicked palms. She ran to the breaker box in full freak-out mode.

Sabrina found the breaker box and reset it, casting the house in a safe, warm light. All the mysterious shapes resettled into regular furnishings. Sabrina chided herself for being so silly. She still had work to do.

Sabrina made her way back upstairs to her bedroom. Even with the lights on, her nerves were still a little on edge. Sure, it was just a circuit breaker, but combined with the weirdness of Scream Site, the strange sound, and the emptiness of the house, it felt like so much more.

Sabrina tried to push her uneasy feelings aside and focus on her mission: Shady99. She sat back down at her desk. Lupe had mentioned that user as the only person who'd had a problem with Mariann, and that seemed as good a place to start hunting for clues as any.

She wondered if maybe Mariann had exaggerated the "harassment" when she'd told her sister about it. Stories were always better with a little embellishment. Even though Shady99's message was seriously inappropriate, Sabrina had been expecting more. It could have just meant that they were coming for her number one slot, not that they were literally coming to get her.

If Sabrina was going to write a story about Scream Site and make it about Internet safety, she had to be able to prove that Mariann's disappearance was tied to the dangers of the site. Was this message enough to suggest that? From what she could see, Shady99 had just messaged Mariann once with some creepiness, and then she'd disappeared. Was that enough to build a case—or a story—on? She was worried that her article would be no better than the silly puff pieces Evelyn liked to read.

Sabrina was beginning to understand why the police hadn't investigated this story any more than they already had. It just didn't add up.

But still, Mariann was missing. Possibly.

Sabrina searched Scream Site again, this time making her way to Shady99's site. When she landed there, a banner proclaimed them "Number One Most Watched User." Indeed, the follower count at the top of the page was nearly a million people, and while most users made a video once a week or so, it looked like Shady99 was uploading something new nearly every day.

"Wow, that's a lot of videos," Sabrina murmured. And as she was looking at the list of videos, a notification popped up stating that there was a new one to watch.

"Well, I guess we might as well start fresh," she whispered. Then she clicked on the newest video and watched as it began to play.

CHAPTER TWELVE

The screen was completely black, and at first Sabrina thought the video was just taking a while to load. But then a faint sound filtered through the speaker. Crying? A girl's voice?

The image slowly came into focus. Like Mariann's video, the picture was grainy, shapes and outlines blurred and hard to distinguish. It looked like the video had been shot at night, the details of the location hard to make out. But then they began to fill in—an empty room with a bare wooden plank floor. A figure in some kind of uniform, like the kind people wore at a fast food place. Shadows, pleading, more creepy nursery rhyme recitations. Fingers clawing at a door that wouldn't open. Eerie, old-timey carnival music. Shrieks of terror.

Sabrina squeezed her eyes shut. She wanted to turn off the video, but she also had to know what would happen.

Sabrina forced her eyes back open. She had to watch this video, but she didn't want to. She covered her face and kept checking the countdown timer to see how long the video had left. On and on it went, the screams, the cruel laughter.

"That is sick," Sabrina said. But even though the video was awful, part of Sabrina didn't know if it was real. This video felt different from Mariann's video. Terrifying, for sure, but was it all an act?

Sabrina took out a notepad and made notes about the video, then scrolled down to see what viewers were saying:

XYZ007: Not as good as the drowning one, but pretty sweet

FanGirl4Ev: Shady is so disturbed. Great videos, they always seem a little too real.

TheWalrus101: much better than the girl from last month

Sabrina clicked on the list of Shady's videos and discovered that they went back four months. Like the user had said, it was a different girl in each month's worth of videos, and there were nearly a hundred videos in total. They all featured a girl from the neck down, her face hidden from the viewer. In some the girl was being chased through the woods. In others the girl was in some creepy storage room, all with dark lighting and weird angles making it difficult to see just what was happening. But in each one, the girl's screams came through loud and clear, raising goose bumps on Sabrina's arms. The identity of the girl was always hidden. No matter how much the girl screamed, there was never a clear shot of her face.

Sabrina watched the videos, stopping most before they were finished. They were too much. If they were fake, these people deserved a movie deal. They were horrifying, and they made Sabrina's skin crawl. All the positive comments talked about how authentic the videos seemed. But what if they *were* real? It doesn't get more authentic than that.

What now?

Sabrina shook her head. "Pull it together, Sebastian," she muttered. There was no way the videos were real. They were fake, just like everything on Scream Site. That was the whole idea, right? The only question was why Shady99 had felt the need to threaten Mariann. Their videos were nothing alike, with Shady99's being much darker. Mariann's earlier videos were all edge-of-your-seat, monsters-in-the-closet kind of stuff. That was part of what made the last video she'd posted so unnerving. By comparison, it was nothing like her earlier ones, and it didn't seem like something she'd post.

Sabrina clicked back to Shady99's most recent video. Something tugged at her mind. There was something about the girl that was familiar. Sabrina opened another window and loaded up Mariann's page. Resizing the windows so that they could play side by side, she played Mariann's last video at the same time as Shady99's new video.

It couldn't be, could it? Maybe she was just imagining it.

Sabrina kept watching, hoping that what she thought she was seeing wasn't true. A few seconds from the end of Mariann's video, Sabrina paused it, doing the same to the video on Shady's site. She stared at the screen, and slowly a chill rolled over her, sending more goose bumps down her arms.

Mariann and the girl in Shady's newest video were wearing the same shoes.

CHAPTER THIRTEEN

Sabrina watched the video two more times before deciding that this was too big for her to handle. This was serious. Those really were the same shoes on both girls, and the girls in both videos were close enough to the same size that she was almost sure it was the same person. Mariann. Sabrina had to find out who this Shady99 was, and why he had Mariann in his own videos now. But how could she track down Shady? After all, like everyone kept reminding her, she was just a kid.

This was the real deal, and it was a matter for the police.

It was getting dark out, but she couldn't wait another minute. Sabrina grabbed a sweatshirt and rode her bike down to the Port Riverton Police Department.

When she walked into the building, the officer on duty recognized her from when she used to come in to visit her dad. He buzzed her in. "Hey kiddo, long time no see. Here to see your uncle?"

Sabrina nodded, and the officer led her back through a maze of desks, some clean, most of them not, to a desk in the corner occupied by an older Black man with a shiny bald head that reflected the overhead lights.

"Hey, John, someone important here to see you," the officer said, giving Sabrina a friendly wink before walking back toward the front office. It had been a while since Sabrina had been to the Port Riverton Police Department. Not since her dad died, in fact. The tangle of memories, inextricably linked to her dad, made her choke up a bit, but she forced the sadness to the side and smiled at Detective Francis.

"Hi, Uncle John."

"Sabrina! What are you doing here, baby girl?" He stood and held his arms open for a hug. Sabrina fell into them gratefully. All the way to the police station, she'd replayed the videos in her mind, seeing them as real, not as silly things created by a bunch of people hoping for their chance in Hollywood. That had made all the difference. She believed real people were being hurt in those videos, people who had gotten caught up in some kind of terrible game. People like Mariann Sanchez.

But now Sabrina was here at the police station and Uncle John would fix it. He would find the person who was posting those videos and make sure they were arrested. He would investigate what she'd found. Sabrina had promised Lupe that she would talk to the police about her missing sister, and Sabrina was going to keep that promise. Maybe she wouldn't get a story out of this whole mess, but she was doing the right thing. Her uncle was the person who could make everything right with the world, just like her dad had done before he died.

All the stress of the things she'd learned about Scream Site began to drain away, and for a moment she was just a little girl again, going to see Uncle John, who always had a pocketful of hard candies to share.

Right on cue, he reached into the top drawer of his desk, pulling out a handful of candy. "Watermelon, grape, or cherry?" he asked.

"Watermelon," Sabrina said with a smile, taking the candy, unwrapping it, and popping it into her mouth. She dropped the wrapper into the nearby trash can before sinking into the chair next to the desk.

Detective Francis sat back down in his chair. "So, this is a nice surprise. What brings you down to the station?"

"I can't just drop by for a visit?" Sabrina asked.

Detective Francis smiled, his teeth bright against the dark skin of his face. "Of course! But I was beginning to think you were holding a grudge, since a certain best friend of yours was mighty sore that I tried to give her a ticket for disturbing the peace."

Sabrina laughed. "Evelyn says hi, by the way."

"Hmph, I bet."

"No, but actually, I need to talk to you about something serious. I suppose you know the name Mariann Sanchez?"

Detective Francis leaned back in his chair, his expression grim. "I do. It's a girl who went missing from right here in Port Riverton a couple weeks back. The question is, why do *you* know that name?"

"Because I was investigating Scream Site for a story, and I think maybe that website has something to do with why she's missing." Sabrina quickly sketched out the details about the videos and the similar girls with their same shoes. She even mentioned her interview with Lupe Sanchez. Sabrina didn't leave anything out, and she realized as she was telling the story that it probably sounded a bit . . . naive. A person stalking girls via a website and then filming them to get likes on his videos? That was the kind of stuff that happened in a movie, not in Port Riverton.

Detective Francis nodded as he listened. His expression was skeptical, but he didn't cut Sabrina off to tell her that she was being silly. "So, you think that this user, Shady99, kidnapped Mariann Sanchez and is now using her to make his videos?"

Sabrina squirmed in her chair a bit. It sounded even more ridiculous when her Uncle John said it like that. "I think there's a good chance that it's the same girl. Have any other girls gone missing in the area? Girls that maybe had Scream Site accounts? Judging from the videos, it appears that there have been at least three other girls besides Mariann since January."

"Why do you say that?"

"Because of the videos. I can show you."

Detective Francis stood up and gestured for Sabrina to take his seat. He was already logged into the Internet via the police network, so she quickly navigated to Scream Site, logging on as a guest rather than signing in to her own account.

He chuckled to himself as he watched her. "I will never get over how quickly you kids have all learned to navigate the Internet."

"I know, I know, you didn't even have the Internet when you were a kid. . . . Here, look: This is Shady99's site."

Sabrina played the video, the one she thought looked like Mariann Sanchez. Detective Francis watched it, grimacing.

"That's terrible. But the girl's face isn't visible. What makes you think it's Mariann?"

"The shoes," Sabrina said, clicking through the video and pausing on a good shot of the girl in the chair, her shoes plainly visible. She then opened a new window and clicked through to Mariann's last video, pausing at the point where her purple shoes could be seen running through the leaves.

Detective Francis rubbed his chin and shook his head. "Yeah, they both have running shoes on. But, isn't the whole point of this website to film scary fake videos? There's nothing here that proves any of it is real or criminal. Besides, we have pretty solid reason to believe that Mariann Sanchez ran away. There's an eyewitness who saw her buying a ticket at a bus station in Baltimore. And friends and family members have corroborated that she had plans to head to L.A. to make it big. She had taken money out of her bank account, so that supports the theory that she had some sort of plan. And she's nineteen. She's entitled to do what she wants."

Sabrina's heart sank. "But why would she be secretive about it? Her sister doesn't think she ran away. And this video is different from anything else she posted. And Shady99 sent her a creepy message—"

Detective Francis raised his hand, cutting Sabrina off. "OK, OK. Even though this case has been reassigned, I'll have another look around the site to see if there's anything suspicious. We did send a couple of inquiries to the site administrators for data, to see if we could trace where Mariann's last video was uploaded from. Just to reassure her sister that she left on her own. And we've spoken to other PD's that have received complaints about the site in the past. All those investigations came back as nothing more than kids making movies, fooling around. Trust me, Sabrina, they're keeping an eye on this. But frankly, detective work takes time. Jumping to conclusions can get us in trouble. But we do take seriously any leads we get on Mariann Sanchez's whereabouts. It's just that, up to this point, the evidence suggests that she left of her own accord. There's no evidence of foul play. She's an adult, and she can leave if she wants— without telling her family, if that's what she wanted.

"And as for creepy messages, we've read them all. Those kinds of messages are exactly why your dad asked you girls to stay off social media, remember? They're everywhere, and, thankfully, ninety-nine percent of the time, they're harmless. Rude and creepy, yes, but nothing more. Listen, it's getting late, and you have school tomorrow. Why don't I give you a ride home, make sure you get there safe?"

Sabrina sighed heavily, deflated after Uncle John's lecture. "But you didn't answer my question. *Have* any other girls gone missing in this area? Any other girls who possibly used Scream Site?"

Detective Francis gave Sabrina a patient look. "There are other unresolved cases, but unfortunately, lots of kids run away—from their families or group homes—or they get caught up with the wrong people or they're trying to stay off the radar. Port Riverton might be a small town, but even here there are tough situations, and sometimes young people make some questionable choices. Or their family circumstances aren't great, so they think they're better off on their own. It's heartbreaking stuff, but I'm afraid a girl leaving town without explanation isn't all that unique."

Sabrina couldn't keep the disappointment and despair off her face. Detective Francis put a comforting hand on her shoulder. "Sabrina, I'm really sorry about Mariann Sanchez. But she's been gone a couple of weeks. Most likely she had her reasons for leaving. It happens. People keep secrets from the people they love. But none of this is your problem. The best thing you can do is just focus on school, on being a teenager, and all that fun stuff. We've all had a rough year after losing your dad. Focus on the good things, OK?"

Sabrina nodded but didn't say anything. Because no matter what Uncle John said, her instincts were telling her that something terrible was happening and that it was all connected to Scream Site.

She was just going to have to figure it out by herself.

CHAPTER FOURTEEN

Uncle John dropped Sabrina off just as her mom arrived home from work. Sabrina wheeled her bike into the garage while Mrs. Sebastian chatted with her brother in the driveway. Sabrina watched from the doorway of the garage as her mom and uncle laughed about something. Was he laughing at her fears about Scream Site? Did he think it was all some big joke? Lupe had said that the police weren't taking the case seriously, and Uncle John's easy manner made Sabrina wonder if Lupe was right. Sabrina certainly didn't feel like laughing right now.

Of course, Uncle John had said that they had

evidence indicating Mariann was OK—that she'd been sighted in Baltimore. If that was true, maybe there was some reason Mariann hadn't wanted to tell Lupe that she was going to quit college and move to Hollywood.

Sabrina watched her mom and uncle talking and thought about how different sibling relationships could be. Mrs. Sebastian and Uncle John talked all the time. He usually called a couple of times a week. It was only their busy schedules that made it so that they couldn't get together more often. Lupe and Mariann had seemed close, at least from the way Lupe talked about her sister, but Uncle John implied that might not have been the case.

Sabrina couldn't help but think about her own sister. She rarely saw Faith other than when she and Evelyn went to Lou's Brews, not even at school. At home they were like ghosts—Sabrina might hear clues that her sister was around from a slammed door or a faucet running or music playing, but they rarely saw each other. She couldn't remember the last time the two of them had sat down and talked. There was their weekly family dinner, but even then there were no heart-to-heart moments, not like there had been before their father died. Now they were living separate lives, and Sabrina realized it bothered her more than she'd thought.

If Faith decided to run away, would she tell Sabrina where she was going? Or would Sabrina be left behind, as hurt and confused as Lupe seemed to be? Sabrina felt a lump rising in her throat. She looked at the empty garage stall where her dad's car used to sit and wished for the millionth time that everything could be liked it used to be.

Uncle John's car pulled away, and Mrs. Sebastian came up the driveway toward Sabrina. "Hey, sweetheart. How was your day?"

Sabrina tensed, wondering how much Uncle John had told her mom. Had he told her that he thought Sabrina was going crazy?

"Fine," Sabrina said, opting to reveal nothing and see what her mom knew.

Mrs. Sebastian nodded. "Your uncle said you stopped by the station because you had a question for an article you're working on. Is this for that internship?"

Sabrina nodded, relief flooding through her. She didn't want her mom to know about Scream Site and the possible missing girls. Mrs. Sebastian would completely lose it if she thought her daughter was involving herself in anything dangerous. And not that Sabrina thought her research was risky in any way, but it never hurt to be too careful.

"Yes, I'm writing about Internet safety. I thought

it would be a good idea to talk to Uncle John about some of the things I found." Not a complete lie.

Mrs. Sebastian entered the house, holding the door open for Sabrina. "Well, that's a good idea, but maybe you shouldn't bother Uncle John at work. He's very busy, you know. Poor guy is drowning in paperwork for petty misdemeanors all the time."

Sabrina nodded. "I know." She paused, trying to decide how to make her escape. "Well, I still have a paper to work on, so I better go do that."

"OK, sweetie. Hey, you haven't seen your sister, have you? She said she had dance team practice tonight, but I thought she would've been home by now."

Sabrina shook her head and ran up the stairs to her bedroom. Her mind once again went to Lupe and Mariann, and Lupe's insistence that her sister wouldn't run away despite the police believing otherwise.

Maybe the truth was just that Lupe hadn't known her sister so well, after all.

CHAPTER FIFTEEN

The next day at school, Sabrina was preoccupied with where to take her investigation next. So much so that it distracted her from everything else she had to do. She completely forgot her homework for algebra, and she almost missed an easy question when Mrs. Wembley called on her in English. Uncle John had told her to focus on being a teenager, and on living life, but it almost seemed that she couldn't remember how to do that.

And part of her didn't want to. She wanted to find out what had happened to Mariann, and to do that, she was going to have to keep asking questions. Sabrina needed more evidence. She'd gone to Uncle John with what she had, and he hadn't been impressed. The next step was obviously to build a better case.

Sabrina had sent Lupe a direct message on Scream Site to ask her what Uncle John had said about Mariann being seen in Baltimore. Lupe's reply had been short: "I keep telling them, that wasn't my sister. That was me. I went to Baltimore to see if anyone had seen Mariann buy a bus ticket. And I didn't buy a bus ticket, just a hot dog from a nearby stand. They don't seem to believe me."

It seemed like a weak explanation, but Sabrina had to admit that she and Faith had been mistaken for each other before too. Sabrina could see the resemblance between Lupe and Mariann, so it was possible that someone had thought one was the other.

Either way, Sabrina believed Uncle John when he said detective work was slow. When her dad was alive, he would sometimes talk to her mom about his investigations over dinner. Many investigations spanned months, and it was only chance that led to breakthroughs most of the time.

" . . . And once we talked to the son, he admitted that he'd faked the robbery to cover for the fact that he'd stolen the money from his mom. That's the thing about working a case. A break usually comes from the most unlikely place. Even something that seems mundane can turn up an important clue," he'd said. He never told them real names or details, of course, but Sabrina loved hearing how he'd solved actual, real life crimes and helped people who needed it. Her dad had made her so proud.

Sabrina felt a fresh burst of inspiration and determination. She knew that she had to investigate every angle, even if it seemed silly and unlikely.

She had to check out Funland, and she needed to find something that linked Mariann Sanchez and her final video to the park. That's where Asher3245 had wanted to meet her. Had Mariann gone there? And what happened if she did?

After the final bell rang, Sabrina tracked down Evelyn. "Hey, do you think your brother would give us a ride out to Funland?" she asked when she found her friend at her locker.

Evelyn frowned. "I thought you said Funland closed? Remember, you heard that it went out of business?"

"It did, but that was apparently where Mariann and her friends shot a bunch of videos. If I'm going to figure out what happened to her, I need to see if I can find the spot where she shot her video."

"Wait, are you talking about tromping through the woods? Hard pass," Evelyn said, making a face. She wasn't a fan of nature, and anything involving wildlife usually made her break out in hives.

"Oh, come on, Evelyn. You owe me, remember?"

"Owe you? For what?" Evelyn asked, scowling as she rooted through her locker for books.

"For the biology project. You know, the one you flaked on?" Sabrina reminded her.

"Oh, come one! You love that nerd stuff," Evelyn whined.

"Yep, but that doesn't change the fact that I had to do it by myself. Plus, this won't be that bad. We know that Mariann shot most of her videos in and around Funland, so it's not like we'll have far to search."

Evelyn shut her locker shut and met Sabrina's gaze. "Let me get this straight. You not only want me to ask my brother to drive us somewhere, but you want to go *into* the woods. And not just any woods—you want to go and figure out which spot of forest was where Mariann Sanchez was maybe murdered? Does this not strike you as possibly the worst idea ever?"

"I didn't say she was *murdered*," Sabrina corrected. "The police seem to think she ran away and is trying to be an actress or something in Hollywood."

"And why don't you believe that?" Evelyn asked.

Sabrina shook her head. "Something is off about this whole thing."

"But you don't think she was murdered? So, what else do you think happened to her? I mean, assuming the video is real. Though I'm still not convinced about that."

"I think it's real," Sabrina said, sticking to her guns. She didn't tell Evelyn that she also thought that whoever had filmed Mariann's final video was maybe now using her to make disturbing horror videos of their own. Telling Evelyn only part of her theory was safer than telling her the whole thing. Evelyn was already looking for an excuse to bail.

Even Sabrina knew that what she was proposing was a bit far-fetched. Trying to convince Evelyn of it as well would take more time than they had.

"Please, Ev. I can't go by myself. You know I'll get creeped out. If you come with me, I'll buy you a chai."

"Why don't you ask Faith to take you? Doesn't she have a car now?" Evelyn asked.

Sabrina gave her friend a long look. "I did. I texted her. No answer."

Evelyn gave Sabrina a sidelong glance. "Are you surprised?"

"No," Sabrina said, dejected, once again thinking about sibling relationships. What would it be like to have a sister she was close to, one who would care about the things happening in her life as much as she did her own? A sudden wave of sadness swept over her. Something must have shown on her face, because Evelyn sighed loudly.

"Chai *and* a muffin," Evelyn said, pulling out her phone.

"Deal," Sabrina said with a grin.

Maybe this time she was finally on a solid lead .

CHAPTER SIXTEEN

Evelyn's brother, Tony, pulled into the parking lot in front of the high school, tires squealing from taking the corner too fast. As he jerked to a stop in front of the girls, Evelyn gave Sabrina a pleading face. "Last chance to run for your life," Evelyn said grimly.

"No way, you aren't getting out of our nature hike that easily," Sabrina said, opening the door and sliding into the backseat while Evelyn climbed into the front. "Hey, Tony!" Sabrina shouted to be heard over the blues music blaring from the speakers.

"Sabrina! Evelyn says you're investigating a murder," he shouted back. Tony Chao had dark floppy hair and thick black-rimmed glasses. He had graduated from high school last year, and Sabrina had always thought he was the absolute coolest. It was only after she got to high school that she discovered most kids thought boys who loved comic books and blues music were not cool. That didn't matter to Sabrina, though. She still thought Tony was awesome.

"It's not a murder," Sabrina shouted back, as a guitar riff wailed through the speakers.

"Right on, girl detective," Tony laughed. "Well, whatever shenanigans are afoot, it's good to know you're on the case." He grinned, putting the car in gear and pulling out of the parking lot. He looked like he was having the time of his life, as usual.

Evelyn did not. She sat in the front seat stiffly, her arms crossed in protest at having to venture into nature. "Did you tell Mom and Dad where we're going?"

"I told them that you had something to do for a school assignment and that I would be playing chauffeur. I might have also said something about you needing to get a driver's license so that I don't have to keep driving you around everywhere."

"Whatever. This was Sabrina's idea. Blame her," Evelyn said.

Tony's eyes met Sabrina's in the rearview mirror.

"Sabrina, if you ever need a ride just let me know. I'm happy to drive *you* anywhere."

Sabrina smiled but didn't say anything. She knew better than to get in the middle of the Chaos' good-natured bickering. Watching Evelyn with her brother sometimes reminded Sabrina again how much she'd lost when her father had died. It felt like she and Faith were further apart than ever now, like their grief had put them on separate islands in a tragic sea. Normally Sabrina tried not to think about it, but it was on her mind a lot lately. And watching Evelyn joke around with her brother brought Sabrina's strained relationship with Faith into sharp focus.

It wasn't far to Funland from school. The park sat just past a couple of farms on the main road out of town. In fact, Sabrina could have ridden her bike. But Evelyn refused to ride a bike outside of town because she was afraid of highways. Skateboard down a set of stairs, sure, but she was chicken on a bike. Getting a ride from Tony had been Sabrina's strategy to make sure Evelyn would come along.

Tony pulled into the gravel parking lot in front of Funland and turned off the car. He pulled out his phone. "All right, you guys have thirty minutes and then this train is heading back to port."

"Station. Trains go to stations," Evelyn muttered, climbing out of the car.

"Whatever," Tony said, already clicking through some game on his phone.

Sabrina climbed out of the car as well and looked around. The park itself sat a little ways back, with a shuttered ticket booth guarding the entrance. From the parking lot, the go kart track and mini-golf course were just barely visible. The outline of the Ferris wheel loomed over it all, frozen in time. All of it had now been fenced off, as if to keep vandals out.

Even though the late afternoon sun was bright, it was difficult to see more than a few feet into the woods that enveloped the park beyond the fence.

Evelyn stood on the gravel, eyeing the woods with disdain. "Well, where to first? The park is literally surrounded by forest."

"Stop being salty. Let's start over there," Sabrina said, pointing to the trees that flanked the right side of the park. "This side seems to have way fewer brambles. And if Mariann was running from her attacker, it makes sense that she would've been running this direction, toward the road."

"All right, but you know it's extremely unlikely that we'll find anything," Evelyn said as they stepped into the tree line.

That was when Sabrina spotted a bit of blue fabric among the leaves on the forest floor.

CHAPTER SEVENTEEN

"Hey, does this look familiar?" Sabrina asked, picking up the blue sweatshirt from the ground. It was dirty and sopping wet, which meant it had been out in the woods long enough to get rained on.

"It's just a gross old sweatshirt," Evelyn said, barely glancing at it and marching forward stubbornly.

"I think this is the hoodie Mariann was wearing in one of the videos. Not that last one, but one of her older videos," Sabrina said, checking the pockets. They were empty. Sabrina dropped the hoodie back on the ground and wiped her hands on her jeans.

"Sabrina, there are like a million blue hoodies in

the world just like that. I have at least three of them myself. Also, I watched that video with you. There is no way in the world to tell what color her sweatshirt was. The video was too dark and grainy. Besides, there's trash all over this place," Evelyn said, looking around at various snack wrappers and pop cans.

"Yeah, maybe," Sabrina said. Evelyn was right. The sweatshirt was gross, and it looked like it had probably been in the woods longer than a couple of weeks.

But still, she stared at the lump of blue fabric and willed it to tell her all of its secrets. Had it seen what happened to Mariann? Were they even in the right place? It all seemed like an impossible task. How was Sabrina supposed to figure out the real deal between Shady99, Asher3245, Scream Site, and Mariann Sanchez when everything looked like a clue to her? And yet none of the clues added up to anything. She was a terrible detective.

Evelyn must have seen the discouragement in Sabrina's face, because she walked back and linked arms with Sabrina. "Let's keep at it. If you want evidence that Mariann went missing in these woods, you're going to need something better than that," Evelyn said.

Sabrina nodded. It was true. She had already gone to Uncle John once. If she went back again, she had to have some conclusive evidence, something that definitely linked everything together.

They walked through the woods, searching for any spots that looked especially disturbed or any trees with twine tied around them, like the tripwire she had seen set up in one of the videos. But after looking for twenty minutes or so, it became clear there wasn't anything to be found.

"Maybe it wasn't these woods?" Evelyn said.

"Maybe. But it looked like this area," Sabrina replied, kicking a rock.

"I guess," Evelyn said. "But all these trees look the same to me. I'm not sure how we're supposed to know which woods are which, to be honest. I mean, as far as I can tell, these trees are exactly like the ones behind your house."

"These trees look nothing like the ones behind my house," Sabrina snapped. But now that Evelyn had mentioned it, she wasn't so sure. Maybe these trees did look familiar because they were the same kind of trees that were in her yard . . . and everywhere in this area.

A car horn blared, and the girls both jumped. "That's Tony," Evelyn said. "He's totally impatient. Come on, you can come to my house for dinner tonight. We're making tacos."

"OK," Sabrina sighed. She and Evelyn trudged

back through the trees toward Tony's car. Her first investigative field trip had been a colossal failure.

Tacos would be just the thing to cheer her up. And maybe help her forget that she wasn't such a great investigative journalist after all.

As they walked to the car, Sabrina tried to push aside her disappointment. She had opened the car door and started to climb in when the tiny hairs on the back of her neck stood up. She paused, turning back toward the woods from which they'd just come. She stared into the trees for a long time, watching for movement or any sign of life.

It felt like someone was watching them.

"Hey, is something wrong?" Evelyn asked, holding the passenger door open.

Sabrina shook her head. "No, I just thought . . . nothing, it's nothing. Didn't you mention tacos?" she said, shaking her head again to clear away her paranoia. She got into the backseat.

"The intrepid investigators are back," Tony said as he put his phone away. "And, FYI, we're having meatloaf tonight, not tacos."

"No one likes meatloaf!" Evelyn complained. "Besides, I already promised Sabrina comfort tacos." She slammed her car door shut as if that ended the argument.

Sabrina smiled as Evelyn and Tony bickered over

dinner options. She stared out the window toward the abandoned front office for Funland. As Tony began to pull out of the parking lot, Sabrina leaned forward, looking closer at a window in the building.

For a moment she almost could've sworn someone was staring back at her.

CHAPTER EIGHTEEN

Sabrina was at a dead end, and her lack of direction put her in a bad mood. She'd been counting on being able to discover where Mariann's final video had been filmed, but she'd failed. She had messaged Lupe about the hoodie, and Lupe confirmed that Mariann did have a blue hoodie. But it was still hanging in her closet. Fail again. And on top of that, Sabrina now owed Evelyn a muffin and a chai.

Sabrina walked through the halls during the passing time between third and fourth period. She had English next with Mrs. Wembley, and she knew that somehow, she was going to have to make up a story about where she was with her article. Mrs. Wembley was expecting her to be handing in a first draft in a few days, and Sabrina had less than nothing—a bunch of questions and zero answers.

For example, why hadn't the police investigated the videos more? From her research there had been multiple reports of people calling the police in order to report that one video or another seemed suspicious. A quick Internet search last night after Sabrina got home had revealed at least six other articles similar to the one that Evelyn had sent her. In one of the articles, a police officer in Michigan was quoted as saying, "We are looking into this matter, and rest assured we take all complaints seriously." Sabrina had even called the police department mentioned, the New Paxton Police Department, and had been told by a woman with a robotic voice that "The department does not comment on ongoing investigations."

Uncle John had said that the Port Riverton police had reached out to other jurisdictions, and that all those reports had come back with nothing. But what if there were others he hadn't checked up on? Regardless, if someone was investigating the website, it meant that other people also thought the videos were real.

There were dozens of disclaimers all over Scream Site, things like "All these videos are for entertainment purposes only" and "No one was harmed in the making of these videos." But that didn't necessarily mean all Scream Site users were following those rules. After all, it wasn't like the Scream Site administrators could possibly verify that each video was "safe."

And so Sabrina came right back to where she started: how to tell if any of the videos were real. And if they were, how to prove it. She'd hoped to prove Mariann's final video was real by finding where it had been shot, and finding some clues to what really happened there and where she might be now. But that had been a bust. Like Evelyn said, there were way too many trees in Maryland to find the few that were in that video. Sabrina needed a different angle.

She had to talk to Asher Grey, the boy who was possibly the last person to see Mariann before she disappeared.

Sabrina didn't know Asher personally, but she knew of him. Mount Clare High School was small enough that pretty much everyone knew everyone else, and everyone especially knew Asher, because he was the kind of boy who could break hearts with a smile. He had corn silk yellow hair that was just long enough to fall into eyes—eyes that Evelyn had once described as "clear blue like a lake on a perfect summer day." She could be quite poetic when there was a cute boy involved. Asher was usually rumored to be going out with a cheerleader at a nearby school or a model who went to the private school, but Sabrina had never seen him dating anyone at Mount Clare.

But Asher wasn't just a pretty face. He was a junior and was president of the Key Club, which spent its time supporting local charities and doing food and clothing drives and generally improving the world. The couple times Sabrina had talked to Asher, he'd been super friendly, which made considering him a suspect in her investigation even harder.

But without any other leads, he was all that Sabrina was left with. Hopefully, he knew something that could help jumpstart her investigation. Otherwise she'd be stuck watching the same awful videos again tonight and banging her head against the keyboard.

After the last bell rang, Sabrina dashed over to the upperclassmen hallway where the juniors and seniors had their lockers. She wanted to catch Asher before he left for the day.

"Hi, Asher, do you have a second?"

Asher looked up from his locker with a smile. "Hey, Sabrina. Of course."

Sabrina tried to not let the fact that Asher knew her name unbalance her. She didn't think anyone knew her name, not really. Freshmen tended to be invisible, but Asher was in the same year as Faith, so maybe he recognized Sabrina because of her. Or maybe he'd read her articles in the school paper.

A zing of pride shot through her, thinking about that, but Sabrina didn't have time to enjoy it. She had some questions for him. She cleared her throat and channeled what she thought of as her serious reporter face: slight frown, pursed lips, like she was super into whatever was being said.

"Great. So, I'm working on a story for the newspaper about this website, Scream Site. There's a rumor that girls have been going missing after using the site, and I was wondering if I could ask you a few questions about it."

Asher's friendly smile disappeared, and he slammed his locker shut. "I don't want to talk about that."

Sabrina paused. Did Asher not want to talk about Scream Site because he knew something or because it brought up terrible memories? Either way, this was a promising development.

She decided there was no use in dancing around the point. Her father had always said direct questions were best once someone became uncooperative. "So then, you know what I'm talking about, that someone used your photo to lure Mariann Sanchez out to Funland? Maybe you know what happened to her?"

Sabrina thought Asher might be her last hope at cracking this case, and she was going all in.

CHAPTER NINETEEN

Asher brushed his hair out of his face and crossed his arms. He wasn't scowling, but it was something like that. It was clear from his body language that he didn't like the turn the conversation had taken. "Yeah, I know. I already spent like an hour answering questions for the police. Look, I'm going to tell you the same thing I told them: I don't use Scream Site, I haven't seen Mariann Sanchez since wood shop class last year, and I wouldn't kidnap anyone. Plus, the day she went missing, I was volunteering at the county animal shelter. Friday nights we always give the dogs baths. Saturday is a big adoption day, and their chances are better if they're clean."

Wow, he sure has the saint thing down, Sabrina thought. But she returned her focus to her questions. "You don't know any users who would go by the handle Shady99, do you? Sometimes people use the same user names across multiple platforms," she said, trying not to get distracted by the mental image of Asher washing adorable puppies.

Asher shook his head. "Nope, not at all. I'm not much into the Internet and stuff. My parents are, uh, kind of strict." Asher's eyes slid to the left, and Sabrina frowned. Did he just lie to her?

Sabrina nodded, like not using the Internet was a completely normal thing. "One last question: Why would someone use your photo? Do you know if Mariann had a crush on you?"

Asher shrugged, looking more uncomfortable. "There was a rumor last year, when she was a senior and I was a sophomore, that she'd told a few people that she thought I was 'adorable.'" He blushed slightly as he said the word. "But that's it. Nothing came of it. I had a girlfriend at the time."

"And do you have a girlfriend now?" Evelyn asked, riding up on her skateboard and butting into their conversation. She kicked it up and tucked it into the space between her backpack and her back, smiling winningly. "Hi, Asher."

"Hey, um, uh—"

"Evelyn," Sabrina said helpfully.

"Evelyn," Asher said. "And the answer is, no, I don't have a girlfriend. Are we finished here? I have to get to my Key Club meeting. We're trying to plan one last food drive before the end of the school year."

"Yes, and thanks for answering my questions," Sabrina said. "It's not that I think you're involved. It's just that there's a girl missing and a sister desperate to find her. And I can't help but think how I would react if it was my own sister." Sabrina felt like that's a how a real reporter would frame it, to capitalize on the sympathetic angle in order to get people to tell as much as they knew. But it was also true. It made her a better investigator to think of it as a personal mission.

Asher's defensive expression melted into one of understanding. "I get it. I really do. And, if I can help with anything else, just ask, OK? But I seriously don't know anything about how or why that girl disappeared, or who sent her my picture. See you later, Sabrina. You too, um—"

"Evelyn," Evelyn said with a sad sigh.

Asher waved and walked down the hall to his Key Club meeting.

"You know, it's super unfair that the cutest boy in school knows your name and can't even remember mine two seconds after hearing it," Evelyn said.

Sabrina sighed too. "I'd be a lot more excited about that if I didn't think he was hiding something."

"Wait, you don't seriously think he's a suspect, do you?"

Sabrina crossed her arms and watched Asher as he joined up with a group of other kids heading to key club.

"Right now, he's my *only* suspect."

CHAPTER TWENTY

Evelyn had to get to her family's store, so Sabrina was left to her own devices. The idea of going home was overwhelmingly depressing. The last thing she wanted was to hang out in her house by herself, stare at Scream Site, and worry about spooky sounds and the lights going out again. So instead she decided to go to the library. Maybe she'd have a case-altering epiphany there. After all, librarians knew just about everything. And if they didn't, they definitely knew how to look it up.

Since she was thoroughly out of leads, Sabrina needed to go back to the beginning and redefine the problem. Instead of wondering if Scream Site was responsible for girls going missing, maybe she should focus on whether it was a pattern—if there were others that had gone missing too. Maybe she could cross reference any girls that had gone missing with users of the website.

If she could find a pattern, that might be enough to make the Port Riverton police and others take notice. They'd have to investigate if she could prove that website was the common denominator in multiple missing persons cases. Uncle John wouldn't be able to dismiss that. Sabrina knew this was an even bigger leap than trying to find out where Mariann's last video had been filmed, but at least she was trying.

Sabrina couldn't bear to sit back and do nothing. She had to keep looking for Mariann Sanchez. She had to because, on the chance that she really was missing, who else was looking for her? Lupe was right. The police had given up before they'd even gotten started. Hadn't Uncle John's little speech said as much? They thought she'd run away. It might be true that a lot of people went missing every year, but Sabrina was beginning to think that not enough people went looking for them.

She wasn't going to give up on them so easily.

The Port Riverton library was in a tiny building

connected to the police station and the rest of the municipal facilities, like the fire station and the mayor's office. This time of day, the library was full of kids doing their homework and parents chasing small children around the picture book section. Sabrina walked through the kids' section and headed to the reference desk, where an elderly, pale-skinned woman with shockingly brilliant dyed red hair and cat-eye glasses read the newspaper.

"Hi, Mrs. Stanford. Can you help me find something?"

The woman put her paper down with a smile. "Of course, dear. It's all bad news, anyway. What do you need?"

"I wanted to know how I could look up all the people who have gone missing in our area over the past few months."

Mrs. Stanford's pressed her lips into a thin line. "Oh, what a grim thing to research. Are you writing something for a research project?"

There was a crash, and both Sabrina and Mrs. Stanford turned toward the magazine racks. Asher was leaning around the back side of it, almost like he was eavesdropping. When he saw them looking, he bent down and hastily began reshelving the magazines. Mrs. Stanford gave him a warning look.

"Yeah . . . for social studies," Sabrina finally said in

response to the question.

"Well, the best way to look that up would be to check out the website for Missing Persons hosted by the Department of Justice. They keep a database that tracks all open investigations into missing persons that's searchable by state. Just log into the reference computer and do a quick search for 'Maryland Missing Persons,' and then you should be able to narrow it down from there. If you get stuck, wave at me and I'll come over and help you."

"Thanks, Mrs. Stanford," Sabrina said.

The librarian stood and hurried over to the magazine rack while Asher apologized profusely.

Sabrina watched the scene with narrowed eyes. What happened to Asher's Key Club meeting? Why wasn't he there instead of at the library, skulking around the magazine rack? She wasn't sure she'd truly considered Asher a suspect in Mariann Sanchez's disappearance, despite what she'd told Evelyn, but now she was on high alert. What did Asher know? And why was he following her?

Sabrina filed the weird behavior away for later speculation and made her way to the reference section's computers. She sat down at the computer on the end, one that gave her a clear view of the rest of the library. Ever since she'd discovered the link between Mariann's last video and Shady99, and since that spooky feeling at Funland, Sabrina had been more than a little on edge, feeling like someone was watching her. Between that and Asher suddenly turning up like a stalker, Sabrina's nerves were jangling like she'd had one too many fancy coffee drinks.

Sabrina took a deep breath and let it out. She put Asher out of her mind and got to work.

Using her library credentials to log in, she did a quick search and found the Department of Justice's website easily. She narrowed the missing persons list she found to women under the age of twenty-five. None of the girls in the videos had looked very old, although it wasn't easy to tell with their faces covered. But there had been something about the girls that made Sabrina think they were all around their late teens or early twenties. Maybe it was the weird uniform they'd all been wearing, or maybe it was their voices.

Sabrina was shocked at the number. The results confirmed there were a total of twenty girls from Maryland who had gone missing since January, when Shady99's videos had started. That included Mariann, whose picture smiled at Sabrina unnervingly from the screen. Sabrina pulled up the locations for each of the girls, eliminating those who had disappeared from towns that were more than an hour away. She decided to start locally at first and then branch out.

When she was done, there were four girls total. The exact same number of girls that were in Shady99's videos. Sabrina had taken notes based on each girl's shoes and body shapes, since their faces weren't visible. She was certain there had been four distinct girls, including Mariann.

This couldn't just be an eerie coincidence, could it?

Sabrina clicked through the details of each of the missing girls, feeling more and more unnerved as she did. None of them were older than 22, and one of them was a student at Bayview Community College, the same school Mariann had gone to.

"This can't be. . . . ," Sabrina whispered.

There was a chiming noise from Sabrina's phone, and she dug in her backpack to see who was texting her. *Family dinner night*, the text said. *Where are you?*

"Oh crap," Sabrina said. She'd totally forgotten. The nights when her mother was home, Faith and Sabrina were expected to be home early for family dinner. Her mom had started the practice when Sabrina's dad was still alive, and it was one of the few traditions that had stuck.

Sabrina saved the information on each girl and dropped it in an email to herself. When she glanced up, ready to leave, she noticed that Asher had left as well. She was going to have to make time to question him about his strange behavior. He'd better have a legit excuse for randomly showing up at the library today. Sabrina didn't like things that couldn't be explained easily, and his behaviors had landed squarely in the realm of suspicious.

But there would be time to wonder about Asher and the missing girls later. For now, Sabrina needed to get home. Her family was waiting.

CHAPTER TWENTY-ONE

When Sabrina walked in the door of her house, the spicy scent of taco meat greeted her. She grinned. Tacos twice in one week? Excellent.

The dining room table was set with bowls of shredded lettuce, cheese, sour cream, and several different salsas. From the kitchen came the sound of old 80s music and Sabrina's mom singing along loudly and off key.

Sabrina dropped her backpack next to the foot of the stairs and made her way into the kitchen. "Hey Mom, is dinner ready?"

Mrs. Sebastian gave her an exasperated look.

"How are you going to run in here and ask about dinner without even giving me a kiss first?"

Sabrina smiled sheepishly and gave her mom a kiss on the cheek. "Hi, how was your day?"

"Good, thank you for asking. And yes, dinner is finished as soon as the refried beans are hot. Why don't you run upstairs and let your sister know? It has been a long week, and I am looking forward to dinner with my girls."

Sabrina nodded and did as her mother asked. Her mom was right—it had been a long week, and she wasn't the only one looking forward to dinner as a family. As much as Sabrina might be embarrassed to admit it, family dinner night was her favorite.

When she got upstairs, Faith's door was closed. Sabrina knocked on it lightly before letting herself in. Faith looked up from her computer.

"Hey? Is dinner ready?"

"Yeah, it's tacos. What are you up to?" Sabrina asked. Faith's sly grin got the best of Sabrina's curious nature.

"Oh, I just uploaded a video. Remember how we were talking about Scream Site? Well, I'd been wanting to give it a try, and after talking about it, my friends and I decided to go for it."

Sabrina sucked in her breath. "Oh, so is this the big secret thing you were working on earlier this week?"

She didn't want to sound so snotty, but Faith's dissing her when she'd asked her for a ride to Funland had stung. And the secrecy about making a silly video was another reminder about just how much Sabrina wasn't up on current events with her sister. She had a vague memory of Faith being interested in making movies once upon a time, but she had no idea she'd actually been doing anything about it. A little part of Sabrina was hurt that Faith hadn't asked her to help.

Faith looked slightly embarrassed. "Yeah, sorry about that. I didn't want anyone to know we were making a video, just in case it turned out awful. But now that it's finished, I'm really excited about it. Here, look."

Faith turned the screen around and showed it to Sabrina. It looked a lot like the other videos on the site. It was Faith running through the woods with a terrified expression, interspersed with cuts of a tall, skinny person in a suit stalking her.

"That's Bridget in one of her dad's suits. Creepy, huh?"

"Yeah. It really is. Great acting," Sabrina said. But she wasn't thinking of the video. She was thinking about Mariann. "Where did you film this? Behind the house?"

"No, out by that old amusement park, Funland. Did you hear it's closed now? A bunch of people were talking about how cool it would be to film a horror movie out there. That Ferris wheel is a super eerie back drop. It gave me the idea to film my video there. I mean, creepy movie on an abandoned mini-golf course? How awesome is that?" Faith sighed. "But no one wanted to get caught trespassing, so we just decided to run around in the woods nearby instead. I think it came out pretty good, though."

Sabrina's heart began to beat faster, and even though Faith was still talking about her friends Bridget and Tiffany and how freaked out they'd been, Sabrina barely heard her. Instead she was thinking about Mariann Sanchez and how she'd disappeared from Funland. If she hadn't run away, if something bad really had happened to her, then Funland was the last place Faith should be, especially if she wasn't aware of the danger.

"Hey, don't you think the video came out really good?" Faith asked. "I mean, I know you don't like scary movies or anything, but I think this is pretty epic."

"Definitely," Sabrina said, unable to pull her eyes away from the screen. The video *was* really good, but she couldn't stop thinking about Shady99 and Mariann Sanchez. And how easy it would be for something to happen to Faith. "It's so creepy."

"Yeah, it would've been even better shot in and

around that rickety windmill on the mini-golf course. Maybe next time we can convince Tiffany to hop the fence. But still, people are going wild for it. I have sixteen comments on it so far! Nice, huh?"

Sabrina's feeling of unease exploded into full-blown panic, and her nerves jangled with alarm. "Hey, just be careful, OK? I mean, that's *you* in the video. What if creepers try to contact you?"

Faith turned the laptop back around and laughed. "I think I know how to deal with some Internet dweebs. Besides, my screen name looks like a guy's name, and I don't have any pics of me on my billboard, so I think it'll be fine." Faith typed a reply to some comment before closing her laptop.

"I know," Sabrina said, "it's just that . . . a girl has already gone missing because of Scream Site. I talked to her sister. There's something seriously weird going on with that website, and it feels like nobody wants to acknowledge it."

Faith plugged in her laptop and frowned at Sabrina. "Wait, this isn't about that story you were doing, is it? About a serial killer using the site to find victims or something?"

"I don't know that it's a serial killer, but something did happen to Mariann Sanchez after she used the site. And I'm worried that other girls may have gone missing after using it too."

"I heard that Mariann Sanchez ran away to Hollywood after talking to some big shot producer. If she was kidnapped, why hasn't the news been all over Port Riverton? I think you're being paranoid, Sabrina. Have you actually been able to connect any of the missing girls to the website?" Faith asked skeptically.

Sabrina looked down at her feet, a hot blush suffusing her cheeks. "Well, not yet, but—"

"You can't go around believing everything you see on the Internet." Faith shook her head. "It's just a fun website. There's nothing sketchy about it. The whole point is that the videos are supposed to look real!"

"Yeah, but Uncle John said—"

"You went to Uncle John about this? Oh man." Faith started to laugh, but not in a way that Sabrina liked. After all, her sister was laughing at her and her idea that somehow girls could go missing just because they used a website. "You know Mom is probably going to give you a lecture about distinguishing reality from make-believe when she hears this."

"I can tell the difference between fact and fiction, Faith," Sabrina snapped, her embarrassment making her temper short. It wasn't as though Sabrina hadn't agonized over the exact same things her sister was saying. But she kept coming back to the feeling that something about Shady99's videos was all too real. She couldn't quite explain exactly what it was. Part of it was the way the videos looked, and part of it was the way the girls on the videos sounded. When they screamed for help, they sounded terrified in a way that people in other videos didn't. You'd have to be a really good actress to sound like that. Even Mariann's final video had a realistic quality that her earlier videos hadn't had. It was different. And it was why Sabrina found it difficult to believe she'd run away. That didn't seem like the kind of video Mariann would've normally posted, and that worried Sabrina. There was an authenticity there that was undeniable.

"Look," Faith said, sobering when she saw Sabrina's irritation, "I'll be careful about using the website, but you have to let this thing go. Write up your article for the school paper and move on. You're just freaking yourself out trying to investigate these Internet rumors. And it's probably just because you've never liked scary stuff—remember what a mistake it was when I made you watch that zombie movie? Seriously. You're worrying over nothing but a bunch of urban legends, and you'll end up a fool if you don't check yourself."

Faith headed out of her room and down the stairs to dinner. Sabrina followed, her shoulders slumped in defeat. The truth was she already felt like a fool.

CHAPTER TWENTY-TWO

Sabrina thought about nothing but Scream Site for the rest of the night, even though she should've been enjoying herself. First there were tacos for dinner, which were her favorite, then a round of board games, since they hadn't played any in a while. Sabrina loved Clue and Monopoly, but she was only half paying attention as they played. Mostly her brain was trying to decide whether everyone was right about giving up on the Scream Site story.

She was no detective; she was just a girl in high school, trying to write an amazing internship application. Maybe she should give up on this idea and write an article about something safe and boring, like the health benefits of avocados. She might be wasting her time chasing this Scream Site thing when she should be working on a hundred other things. Hadn't she already forgotten her algebra homework earlier this week? She had to get her life back on track.

And she told herself she should probably just forget about Asher Grey. Did she really think a boy she went to school with could have anything to do with a missing girl? And how exactly would he have orchestrated such a feat in between volunteering at animal shelters and being star student at school? It didn't make any kind of sense.

Maybe it was all just a massive coincidence. It was possible Mariann had run away, as everyone but her sister seemed to believe. And maybe someone had used a random picture of Asher Grey from some website. Sabrina might only be seeing anything suspicious because she wanted it to be some kind of big conspiracy—because it would be a journalist's dream scoop. Her brain told her she should focus on a different story, one that would actually turn out to be something more than just a bunch of random gossip based on guesses and hunches.

But her gut told her something else.

She couldn't stop investigating. Even if it was all a hoax, it could still be a great story for her application, and it would prove that she could follow a lead to its conclusion. And, if the Scream Site rumors were true and Mariann Sanchez had been kidnapped because of the website, then there were real lives at stake, and that was much more important than any internship.

So then the question was: What next?

Sabrina went back and forth over all this during the night of family fun, all the way until she drifted off to sleep, and again as she went through her classes the next day, including Wembley's fourth hour English class.

"Sabrina, how is your story coming? The one on Terror Site?" Mrs. Wembley asked after class, just as Sabrina was about to step outside the door.

Sabrina's slouched and turned back around to face her. "It's going OK," she said, the lie making her stomach knot.

Mrs. Wembley smiled, the corners of her eyes crinkling. She looked more energized today, and it made Sabrina feel a little less bad for lying to her. She wouldn't want to be the one to disappoint Mrs. Wembley.

"Well, do you have a few minutes to tell me about it?" Mrs. Wembley asked. Sabrina bit back a sigh. Mrs. Wembley knew she did—it was lunch period. Sabrina had exactly forty-five minutes until her next class.

Mrs. Wembley indicated a chair and Sabrina shook

her head. "I'll stand, thanks." Hopefully by not getting comfortable, she could make a quicker escape.

"No problem. So, Terror Site?"

"Scream Site. And my investigation is going OK, like I said. I've mapped out several different leads about the dangers surrounding the website, and the most prominent one seems to be about girls going missing after using the website."

Mrs. Wembley frowned. "Investigation? What do you mean?" Her voice went up in pitch, her eyebrows raised in alarm. Sabrina silently cursed to herself. The last thing she needed was a teacher knowing that she'd been trying to figure out what had happened to a real kidnap victim. Mrs. Wembley would call her mom and then there would for sure be no more chasing down any possible leads, and that meant definitely no article.

And without this article there would be no *Daily Sun* internship. That was for certain.

"Uh, just research," Sabrina said, shifting from foot to foot. Her brain darted back to Faith's accusation last night about believing urban legends, and she decided to use that to her benefit. "I've been looking into some urban legends about the website, to see how they tie into general Internet safety concerns. Sort of how the old fairy tales are really cautionary tales. I've been researching rumors and Internet myths to see what it is they can teach us about being savvy Internet users." None of this was true. Sabrina hadn't been thinking about urban legends as cautionary tales at all. She'd been completely focused on figuring out what had happened to Mariann Sanchez. But now that she'd made up such a story for Mrs. Wembley, she realized it wasn't such a terrible idea after all.

"I've been cross referencing the various urban legends with ones that are popular on other, similar websites. Things like identity thieves stalking the boards, people joining online cults, that sort of thing. It's amazing how much these rumors appear across the Internet," Sabrina finished, tying the lie up with a pretty bow and hoping Mrs. Wembley bought it.

The alarm faded from Mrs. Wembley's face. "Oh, that sounds intriguing. And much less dangerous than *investigating* does. As your teacher, I simply couldn't allow you to be probing into potentially violent crimes."

Sabrina forced a laugh and shook her head. "No, no crimes Mrs. Wembley. Just rumors. And a lot of Internet searching."

Mrs. Wembley nodded. "That's what research tends to be, unfortunately. A lot of looking for that one crucial detail that connects seemingly unrelated things. I will say, the idea of shared stories is a great angle. Narratives do have a way of repeating themselves across cultures and locations, such as the presence of a Snow-White type fairy tale in just about every cultural tradition. Have you decided how you're going to incorporate these findings into your overall story?"

"Not quite." Sabrina just wanted to exit the conversation. And besides, it wasn't like she was really writing about any of this. Her plan was still to find out what had happened to Mariann Sanchez. Mariann's disappearance was the centerpiece of her story, and discovering what had happened to her was the most important thing. "I'm sorry, I have to get going before the lunch line closes," Sabrina said, adding another lie to her list, since she had packed her own lunch that day. Very little of what she'd said had been the truth, and Sabrina wasn't a natural liar. In fact, she was pretty terrible at it, which was why she was a reporter and not a creative writer. It was only a matter of time before Mrs. Wembley asked the right question and the truth came pouring out.

And that would be disastrous.

"Oh, of course," Mrs. Wembley said with a friendly smile. "I don't want to take up your lunch period. Just let me know if you need any help. I'm really looking forward to this article."

Sabrina nodded and escaped the classroom before her guilty conscience gave her away.

CHAPTER TWENTY-THREE

Sabrina tried to put her guilt aside during lunch, and she was mostly successful. Evelyn had a ton of new gossip to share and the tater tots Sabrina grabbed from Evelyn's tray were perfectly done—crispy on the outside and yummy on the inside. Just what she needed right now. For nearly thirty whole minutes, she was completely engaged in the moment, not thinking about Scream Site at all.

But all that changed when she sat down in the computer lab for her club period. Every six days in the schedule a separate hour was set aside at the end of the day just for clubs. Every student was supposed to pick a club to go to, as part of what the school called "cultural enrichment." Evelyn had chosen Pokémon Club, and if Sabrina looked out of the front window during club times, she could usually see Evelyn and other members of the Pokémon Club walking around like zombies and staring at their phones. To Sabrina it seemed like the silliest club ever, but Evelyn loved it.

Sabrina had chosen Journalism Club, naturally, which was really just an extra hour that she got to work on her newspaper articles.

Today she was using the time to study the data she'd pulled on the girls missing from the area. She still felt bad about lying to Mrs. Wembley, but she had to find her next lead, and doing that meant she was going to have to figure out if more than just Mariann Sanchez had possibly gone missing because of Scream Site.

When she'd first downloaded the information about missing people, Sabrina had assumed she might only use it in the article as a factoid, to provide context for how often missing persons cases happen in general.

But as Sabrina looked at the information, she realized her deep-down suspicions had been right all along: Scream Site wasn't just a website that might be *connected* to a couple of disappearances—it was the reason those local girls had disappeared. And when she saw the dates, a prickle of certainty ran across her skin.

Cicely Jones had gone missing in January, Rae-Ann Jackson disappeared in February, and Georgia Fanus was last seen in March. Then in April, it was Mariann. Their dates of disappearance were each about a month apart, give or take a few days. That seemed odd, almost like they were on some sort of schedule. That coincidence alone seemed weird enough that the police should have taken note.

Sabrina wondered why she hadn't heard anything about these women going missing in her area. Had she just not been paying attention to the news? Or was something else at play, here? All the victims were over eighteen, and Sabrina wondered if that had made the police less likely to worry about them. Still, it was enough to set off all Sabrina's alarms.

"This is weird," Sabrina murmured aloud. She tried to log into Scream Site web, but it was one of the many sites that were blocked on the school's Internet. Instead she jotted down a few notes to herself so she could look at the website later, including searches for the missing girls' names to see if they had accounts. She also texted Uncle John. She wanted to ask him about these, to see if he'd discuss any details with her. Probably not, but it was worth a try.

"Hey, Sabrina, can I talk to you?"

Sabrina jumped and turned around. Asher Grey was standing behind her, a sheepish smile on his face. It was strange to see him popping up in another place where she wasn't expecting him. She wondered if Key Club was using the computer lab to print flyers or something.

"I'm kind of busy right now, Asher," Sabrina said, covering up the printouts she'd been looking at. He still didn't fit her mental image of a kidnapper slash creepy video maker, but from what she'd learned on TV, you never can tell. Isn't it always the ones you least suspect? For now, she would be on guard around him.

"It'll only take a minute," Asher said.

Sabrina swiveled her chair around so she was facing him. "Fine. What's it about?"

"Your Scream Site investigation. I feel like our conversation yesterday didn't go so hot, and I wanted to explain," he said. He looked worried. But was he worried that Sabrina might think he had something to do with Mariann Sanchez's disappearance, or that she might find out something he didn't want her to know?

Whatever it was, Sabrina was intrigued.

"You have some info about my investigation?"

Asher nodded, his head bobbing nervously. "It's about something the cops told me. I'd rather talk about it out in the hall, if you don't mind."

She shrugged, playing it casual. Nothing could happen in the middle of the school hallway, right? She was safe enough talking to him, she hoped. "Fine with me."

Sabrina stood and followed Asher out into the hallway. The space was empty and curiously quiet, the hum of voices and keyboards from inside the computer lab fading into the background.

"OK, so I didn't want to say anything earlier, because I was hoping this would all go away . . . but I don't think Mariann Sanchez was the only girl to go missing," Asher said, pushing his hair back from his face.

Sabrina blinked, turning Asher's words over in her mind. This was exactly what she'd been looking for—some kind of confirmation of what she suspected too. She needed a tangible direction to search in, some kind of guidance. And here was Asher, giving it to her freely. It was perfect.

Too perfect.

"Why do you think that?" Sabrina asked, trying to temper her excitement. She had to focus, to be skeptical and inquisitive like a good journalist would.

Asher glanced up and down the hallway and

lowered his voice. "There were pictures of other girls, and the cops asked me if I knew them too. They didn't tell me why they were asking, but I figured it's because something happened to them as well."

Sabrina nodded, collecting her thoughts. She didn't want Asher to know just how much she knew. "Did they give you any names?"

"No, but they asked me if I knew any of the girls from either Lou's Brews or Funland."

"Why would they ask you about Funland?" Sabrina asked with a frown. In the back of her mind, she remembered that Evelyn had mentioned seeing Asher there. And she remembered Asher3245's invitation to meet Mariann there.

Asher ran his hand through his hair. "I worked there. Over the summer. It was terrible, and I wouldn't recommend it to anyone. People were always mad that the Ferris wheel was broken, and I never got paid on time. But I didn't know any of the girls they showed me, and I didn't want to ask who they were, if they even would have told me. But they asked me all these questions while they were interviewing me about Mariann, so I figured all those girls must have disappeared out at Funland or something." Asher's expression darkened, his pale brows knitting together. "Before you ask, I didn't have anything to do with *those* girls going missing, either. And I still don't know how my picture got up on the message board. That really creeps me out."

Sabrina took a deep breath and let it out. She felt a glimmer of sympathy for him. But more importantly, this confirmed that there were other girls possibly involved, and that they all had something in common—Funland. And Funland pointed back to Scream Site.

Now she needed to talk to Uncle John more than ever.

But she wasn't done with Asher yet. "OK, that makes sense, but I have another question for you: Why were you eavesdropping on me at the library last night?"

"I wasn't! I had a paper to research. It was totally a coincidence that you were there. Sorry, I knew it probably looked like I was following you. I lied to you about having a Key Club meeting to . . . avoid you, I guess, and then I sort of got caught in my lie when you saw me at the library. That's why I wanted to tell you the part about the other girls, because I hate keeping secrets. And lying." He made a face. "Anyway, I swear I've told you all that I know."

Sabrina watched Asher for a long minute, waiting for some sign that he was lying. But she couldn't tell. She wasn't like one of those girls in a mystery who always knew when someone was lying. She was just following the facts as she went, and hoping the instincts she did have weren't leading her wrong.

The bell rang, signaling the end of the school day. Sabrina gave Asher one last look. "Thanks for telling me," she said. She didn't completely trust him yet. After all, the fact that he'd worked at Funland all summer definitely gave him some insider knowledge about that property. But if he was telling the truth, he was in a tough position too. Someone had posed as him in order to potentially commit a very serious crime. Somehow, his face and his name had gotten caught up in this. If he wasn't responsible for those girls going missing, someone had sure done a good job of setting it up to look that way.

Uncle John had said that they'd reached out to Scream Site to get the time of Mariann Sanchez's last upload. Had they also looked for other things, like the IP address of Shady99? And of Asher3245? And if so, what had they found?

Sabrina unraveled each thread in her mind.

"See ya," Asher said and walked down the hall to his locker. Sabrina went back into the classroom and sat down at her computer. Now that she knew there were other girls that the police were asking about, she had even more questions than before.

But when she got back to her computer, all her information was missing. The sheets she'd printed out and highlighted were nowhere to be found, along with the notes she'd made about Shady99.

Someone had stolen all her research about the missing girls.

CHAPTER TWENTY-FOUR

On the way home from school, Sabrina stopped by the library and printed out her information once more. This time it went much faster, because she knew what she was looking for. But that didn't make the disappearance of her work any less strange.

No one in the computer lab seemed to know where her stuff had gone. She'd asked everyone, even the kids sitting at tables nowhere near the computers. Had someone accidentally picked it up with their own work? Or had it gotten swept into the recycling?

Or maybe someone had taken her information on the missing girls, and maybe Asher had been distracting her while they did it.

Whatever happened, it was annoying and more than a little troubling.

When she got home, she hear loud music coming from upstairs, a sure sign that Faith was home. That made Sabrina feel a little better. But she couldn't shake the feeling that someone had deliberately taken her research. And then there was that feeling that she was being watched. Sabrina didn't consider herself the paranoid type, but she was starting to wonder if someone didn't want her poking her nose into these matters. Both Mrs. Wembley and Uncle John had been worried because it was dangerous, and maybe they were right. It seemed like someone really didn't want her to find out anything more about the missing girls.

Sabrina grabbed an apple from the kitchen before heading upstairs. Now that she knew the names of the girls, she wanted to see if any of them had Scream Site accounts. If she could somehow connect them to Scream Site, then Uncle John would have no choice but to listen to her theory.

Speaking of Uncle John, he still hadn't returned her texts asking about the Mariann Sanchez case. Sabrina called him, but his phone went straight to voicemail, so she left a message.

"Hey, Uncle John, it's Sabrina. I'm calling about the Mariann Sanchez case again. I know you think that Scream Site isn't involved, but I was wondering if you could tell me about these other missing persons cases I found in our area. I know you probably didn't handle them because they didn't happen in Port Riverton, but I've heard that they might all have a Funland connection. Which seems odd. Anyway, love you and miss you, and I hope you're being safe."

Sabrina hung up, feeling something between anxious and excited. If Uncle John had information he was holding out on her, she just wanted him to tell her if she was hot or cold—if she was on the right track or so far off track that she needed to completely rethink the whole investigative reporter thing. Sabrina wanted to be right, but she was also afraid what it might mean if she were.

After all, Faith still used Scream Site. And if someone was using Scream Site to target girls, that meant Faith could be in danger.

Sabrina took a deep breath and pushed the thought aside. She had to focus on the most pressing matter at hand, and that was tying the list of missing girls to Scream Site accounts.

Sabrina logged into Scream Site quickly, checking her messages first. There was nothing, as usual, so Sabrina took a deep breath and clicked the search box.

She was trying to find the first girl, Cicely Jones, when Evelyn called.

"Hey," Sabrina answered, scrolling through user names for any that could possibly be Cicely.

"I'm booooored," Evelyn said. "I have to be at the store until seven and it is dead. What are you doing?"

"Trying to match up the girls who went missing from our area to Scream Site accounts."

"Ummm, why?"

"Because I think that someone might be stalking girls who make videos on Scream Site and kidnapping them and then using them to make their own videos," Sabrina said, matter-of-factly.

There was a moment of silence on the line before Evelyn said, "What?"

Sabrina took a deep breath, and then quickly caught Evelyn up to speed. "There's a weird trend of girls going missing who seem to have some connection to Funland. I found the girls' names from an online database."

Sabrina could almost feel Evelyn's disapproval across the line. Evelyn thought Mariann Sanchez had run away, just like everyone else. But she didn't remind Sabrina of that. Instead she just asked, "So, how's it going?"

Sabrina sighed. "So far nothing. I guess there's no way to match real names to profiles?"

"Hmm, probably not. For privacy reasons or whatever. Can you tie them to the website some other way?"

"Like how?" Sabrina asked, eager to have someone else taking an interest in helping her.

"I don't know, maybe try to figure out if the girls in the Shady videos are the same as the missing girls?" On the other end of the phone came the sound of a bag opening and Evelyn crunching through some snack.

"Hmmm. Yeah, maybe I can find something in the videos that identifies the missing girls," Sabrina replied.

"Yeah. And, if you can't find accounts for the girls by their names, I wonder if you could narrow down users based on their location. Just do a search using 'Maryland' or something?"

"Good idea. I'll try. Ugh, detective work is so slow. It always looks so exciting and fast-paced in the movies," Sabrina said.

Evelyn laughed. "Movies are full of lies! If this were a movie, you would've solved the case with one random clue and fallen in love with the killer by now."

Sabrina laughed. "So true. Hey, I have to tell you about this weird thing that happened to me today." Quickly Sabrina filled in Evelyn on Asher's confession and her missing documents.

Evelyn said nothing for a long while before saying, "That's super weird, Sabrina."

"I thought so too. I have to talk to Mrs. Wembley about my story again tomorrow, just to give her an update. Do you think I should mention it?"

"Didn't you just talk to her about it?"

Sabrina sighed. "I did, but she's keeping close tabs on me. I lied because I didn't want her to know I was investigating a bunch of possible kidnappings. I think she's on to me, though."

"You hate lying," Evelyn said, her voice full of concern.

"I know, but I had to lie to cover. This is really important to me, and I am so far behind. I was supposed to turn in a draft already, and since I have shown her nothing, she's getting really anxious."

"She's not the only one," Evelyn said.

"What's that supposed to mean?" Sabrina asked, trying not to get defensive.

Evelyn snorted. "Exactly what you think it means. I think you should stop all this craziness."

Sabrina stopped clicking through the Scream Site website and gave the conversation her full attention. "Wait, what?"

"Sabrina, this is getting out of hand. Let's just say that someone really *is* kidnapping girls that they find through a website. That's creepy enough by itself. But now you might be the only person who knows about it. Don't you see what kind of serious danger you'd be in if that were true? Especially if Asher *is* somehow involved? He knows everything you know, plus he could totally be the one who stole your information. What if his heartfelt confession was just a way to find out how much you know?"

Sabrina's stomach churned with dread. "You think he would have done that?"

"No, because I can't possibly believe that about my future husband, but *if* he is a psycho killer kidnapper dude, they're really good at lying and pretending to act all innocent, right? I mean, you've seen all the same shows I have. You don't know what creepos might be capable of if they suspect that someone has found out their secrets," Evelyn said, her tone even and completely reasonable.

As Evelyn talked, Sabrina felt a horrible tingle run up her spine. Was someone investigating *her*?

"So, you really think I should ditch the whole investigation?" Sabrina asked. She propped the phone between her ear and her shoulder and rubbed her hands up and down her arms to get rid of the sudden goose bumps.

"Oh, definitely," Evelyn said. "But I know you won't. So here's what you should do instead: Find something compelling enough that convinces your super cool detective uncle to take up the case. Because if you don't, you could be next on the Scream Site psycho's list."

CHAPTER TWENTY-FIVE

After hanging up with Evelyn, Sabrina was even more determined to see if she could try to connect the girls to Scream Site. Not just because she was scared, which she definitely was after hearing Evelyn's well-reasoned point of view, but because she wanted the person who had made all those videos to be stopped.

What Evelyn had said about someone coming for Sabrina really freaked her out. If the videos were real, then once the person making them figured out Sabrina was investigating, they would probably do something to get her to stop.

But to prove those videos were real, Sabrina had

to prove that the person who had made them was responsible for the disappearances. And it was pretty obvious that there was no way she was going to be able to do it by searching the site, trying to find out if the girls had profile pages. That was going nowhere. So Sabrina went back to the one constant in the whole case.

Shady99.

Shady's videos were the horrifyingly realistic ones. And Shady had been the only person to threaten Mariann Sanchez before she disappeared. And a few days after Mariann's uber scary final video was posted to her billboard, Shady99 posted a video featuring a girl who looked a lot like Mariann. Shady99 also had videos featuring different girl "actors" each month . . . and it just so happened that other girls had gone missing each of those months.

If anyone was responsible for everything that was happening, it had to be Shady99. Whoever that was.

Mariann had received the threatening message from Shady a few days before going missing. Maybe Shady had done this before with other girls on the site, and had messaged them as well?

Sabrina went to the magnifying glass at the top of the website and searched for Shady99's user name. The first few hits were either videos posted by Shady99 or comments on Shady99's videos. Sabrina kept scrolling, amazed at how popular Shady99's videos were. More often than not, they were the video of the day.

After scrolling through several pages, Sabrina moaned, "This is impossible." There were too many search results for Shady99, most of them were comments directed toward Shady, not from Shady. This user was way too popular. It would take forever to find something that might be related to the missing girls without any other information to go by.

Sabrina leaned back in her chair with a sigh. If Scream Site was the common denominator between all the missing girls, then it made sense that they'd all had similar experiences on Scream Site. So, maybe if Sabrina could recreate Mariann's experience, she could stumble across another way to find the pages of the other girls.

Sabrina got a piece of paper and began making a list of the things that had happened to Mariann:

—*Mariann joins Scream Site in order to pursue her dream of becoming a director.*

—*Mariann makes several videos, a few of them at Funland in the woods where lots of people shoot scary clips.*

—*Mariann's video is the most clicked on and voted top video of the day.*

—*Mariann gets threats from lots of different people,*

according to Lupe. But only the threat from Shady99 is on her account.

—Cute boys comment on Mariann's popular video. One of them is Asher3245. They message back and forth and agree to meet to shoot a video. Asher Grey claims it wasn't him.

—Mariann disappears without leaving a note.

—Everyone believes that Mariann ran away because of her dreams of stardom. Lupe says that's not true.

Sabrina looked at the list and circled the things that could be traced to Scream Site. She couldn't find the other girls' videos without knowing their user names, and she wouldn't know if there were threats against them or if they went to Funland until she found their pages. Sabrina's eyes locked on the third item on her list. Mariann's video had been number 1. What if that was what these girls had in common? That they had each knocked Shady out of the top spot at some point?

Sabrina clicked back to the landing page for Scream Site and clicked on the banner for the video of the day. To the right there was an archive of the number one videos of the day going all the way back to the day Scream Site was launched, nearly a year ago.

Sabrina checked the date the first girl, Cicely Jones, had gone missing. January twenty-third. Sabrina clicked back to January first and began going through the daily videos to see if anything stood out in the days leading up to her disappearance.

Luckily, she didn't have to go far. The top video on January third starred a blond girl that looked a lot like the picture of Cicely from her missing poster. And when Sabrina clicked on the billboard of FLirtyGurl23, the user who posted the top video, she found an exact duplicate of the photo on Cicely Jones's missing poster.

"Bingo," Sabrina said, feeling a scary kind of excitement. She'd found her first link between Scream Site and the other missing girls. Now, she just had to find a way to connect the rest and convince Uncle John that she was right.

Then maybe she could finally get the police to give Scream Site the attention it deserved.

CHAPTER
TWENTY-SIX

Sabrina could barely keep her eyes open through English class the next day. She'd stayed up all night trying to find Cicely, Rae-Ann, and Georgia on Scream Site. She'd only been partially successful. There was a profile that could have belonged to girl number two, Rae-Ann Jackson, but Sabrina wasn't really sure. And she couldn't find anything that even looked remotely close to girl number three, Georgia Fanus. Still, Sabrina had kept digging until she'd watched most of the number one daily videos in the months each of the other girls had gone missing. Thank goodness it was only three months' worth. Sabrina couldn't handle much more fake blood, fake screams, and fake fear. And forests. Everyone shot their videos in the woods. She would never look at trees the same way again.

Even though they were number one picks, most of the videos were kind of cheesy and pretty clearly fake. But that was better than watching the horribly realistic ones Shady99 posted. And comparing all Shady99's horrifying videos to the fake-looking ones made Sabrina even more convinced that Shady99's *were* real. They had an authenticity, a level of emotional realness that none of the other videos had. There was a reason the Shady videos plagued Sabrina's dreams. Because seeing real danger left a mark. And so did worrying about the missing girls. What had happened to them? And where were they now?

The bell rang, startling Sabrina out of her doze. Two more classes and she'd be done for the day. She planned on heading over to the police station to share her new discoveries with her Uncle John, hoping that maybe this time he'd take her seriously. He still hadn't returned any of her calls or texts, and while Sabrina wanted to believe he was just busy, she also had a feeling he was brushing her off.

She wasn't surprised. The idea that a website could be the reason several girls had all gone missing was really far-fetched. She got that. Uncle John probably didn't want to indulge her wild imagination. But once she had all the evidence and documentation for him, he would have to believe her. Or at least have to look into it. And, at the very least, Sabrina was pretty sure she had more than enough material to write an amazing article.

But that wouldn't save Mariann Sanchez, wherever she was.

If she was even still alive.

Sabrina had almost escaped out the door when Mrs. Wembley called her back. "Sabrina! How's the article coming along for Scary Site?" she asked.

Sabrina cringed, then turned and stood aside to let the other students exit before making her way to Mrs. Wembley's desk. *Here we go again*, she thought. "It's Scream Site, Mrs. Wembley. And good. It's gotten interesting." Sabrina didn't say anything further.

"Well, I hope you're going to have a compelling article for me by next week. This is going to be the final regular issue of the school paper. After this one it'll be all retrospectives for the seniors who are graduating. If you want to get an article published to use for the *Daily Sun* internship, this will be your last chance."

Sabrina nodded. In all honesty, the internship was the furthest thing from her mind lately. She'd been so focused on solving the mystery. "Oh, it's going great, Mrs. Wembley. And I think my article is really going to set me apart from the rest of the competition. I've managed to tie at least two missing girls to Scream Site, and I'm working to find connections for the two others."

Mrs. Wembley's face twisted into a frown. "Missing girls? Are you back to that, Sabrina? I thought you were writing about the commonality of urban legends and the persistence of cautionary tales in an online environment."

Sabrina blinked. Mrs. Wembley had a habit of using confusing words when simple ones would do, especially when she was all worked up. It took her a moment to translate the words into something meaningful. "I was writing about urban legends and how they exist in online spaces, but then I discovered credible evidence that this website is somehow tied to some unsolved disappearances. I think that's a more interesting story—how a website that's fun could also have an incredibly dark side."

"This is very concerning, Sabrina," Mrs. Wembley said, straightening a pile of papers on her desk. "If this person on the website truly is kidnapping people, then the police should be involved. You shouldn't be running around trying to investigate real crimes."

"I know. I'm going to the police station after school to give them the information I have so far."

Mrs. Wembley nodded, but still looked concerned. "Be careful. If wrong person finds out that you've been digging around, well, you don't know what could happen. Please just write your article with whatever information you already have and leave the kidnapping investigations to the professionals."

Sabrina nodded. Mrs. Wembley was right. She needed to get the real detectives involved before something happened to her. Everyone kept telling her how dangerous her investigation was. From the safety of her desk chair, it didn't really feel dangerous, but it was probably a matter best left for the police. After all, she was just a high school freshman trying to get an internship. Not risk her life.

Hopefully someone would find out what happened to Mariann Sanchez and the other girls. It just wouldn't be Sabrina.

CHAPTER TWENTY-SEVEN

Sabrina left Mrs. Wembley's class and headed to her locker. On the way there she passed Asher. He had a stack of papers in his hands and was reading them with a frown. He looked up and saw Sabrina, his eyes widening for a moment before he composed himself.

"Hi, Asher," Sabrina said, glancing at the papers in his hand. What was he reading that was giving him such a strange expression?

"Hey, Sabrina." He had a guilty face, and he tried to hide the papers from her, which just made her even more interested in seeing what they were.

"What are you reading?" Sabrina asked.

"Um, something someone jammed into my locker. Some printout about missing girls." He reluctantly showed them to Sabrina, and now it was her turn to be surprised.

Asher was holding Sabrina's research notes on the missing girls—the research that had been stolen yesterday, complete with the notes she had jotted on them.

"Those are mine," Sabrina said slowly. "I was using them for research about my article."

Asher held the papers out to Sabrina. "Here, take them. You'll probably want your notes. I'm guessing you weren't the one who put them in my locker?"

Sabrina shook her head and took the papers from him. She already had the information she needed from them, but she didn't really want those loose in the school hallways. She had scribbled quite a few notes on them.

Asher still frowned. "What?" Sabrina asked him.

He sighed. "I don't know. It's just been kind of a weird few weeks. First my picture shows up on some missing girl's message board, then I'm getting interrogated by the police, and now this. It's like someone is trying to frame me or something."

Sabrina gave Asher a sympathetic look. "I'm sure

it'll be fine," she said, hoping she sounded convincing.

But what she was really thinking was that it *did* look a whole lot like Asher was guilty of something the more time went on.

"Thanks for getting these back to me," Sabrina said. She unzipped her backpack and stuffed the papers inside.

"Yeah, no worries," said Asher, looking very worried. Her gave Sabrina a small nod before walking off, and she continued on to her locker.

Sabrina tried to quiet the little voice in her mind that wondered how Asher had come by her notes. She wasn't sure the answer would be anything good. Sure, maybe he really had found them. Or maybe he'd had someone steal them.

Sabrina needed to figure out who was responsible for the Shady99 account. She realized she wasn't ready to give up the investigation quite yet after all.

* * *

After school, before heading over to the police station, Sabrina went by the Gas and Go to see Lupe Sanchez. She'd messaged her earlier in the day because she wanted to touch base with her one last time before she turned over everything she'd found to the police.

Sabrina parked her bike outside and made her way into the gas station. More than just a place to buy gas, Gas and Go was busy, with customers lined up for fried chicken and sandwiches as well as the usual convenience store staples. Their food wasn't as good as Lou's Brews, but they were open twenty-four hours, and a lot of people stopped in for coffee or food when they were in a hurry. Most of the high school crowd headed to either Lou's Brews or Gas and Go for an afterschool snack, so Sabrina was walking in the door at one of the busiest times of the day.

Lupe wore a Gas and Go shirt and a baseball cap. She worked one of the registers and waved to Sabrina when she came in. "I have my break in ten minutes. Wait for me in the back," she called while ringing up a gallon of milk and a couple boxes of cereal for a harried-looking older woman. Sabrina nodded and made her way to the back of the store, where a few sticky tables were arranged haphazardly in front of the hallway to the bathrooms.

While she waited, Sabrina rehearsed in her mind what she wanted to say to Lupe, so that she wouldn't stumble when it was time to talk. When Lupe slid into the chair across from her, Sabrina was ready.

"OK, so I've found out a lot since we last talked," Sabrina began.

"But not my sister," Lupe said, voice flat. Sabrina tried not to wince. Already off to a rough start.

"No, but what I did discover is that she may be

part of a larger pattern of girls going missing. I've created a report that I'm going to take to the Port Riverton police," Sabrina said, sliding a stapled stack of papers across the table to Lupe. "I'm hoping it'll be enough for them to consider Mariann's disappearance as a possible kidnapping rather than a runaway. Since there are other girls involved, they should reach out to those jurisdictions as well, which would mean more people looking."

Lupe furrowed her brow at the report, her expression somewhere between hope and resignation. "Mariann has been gone for almost a month. I read that the more time that passes before a kidnap victim is found, the less likely it is that they *will* be found." She slid the report back across the table to Sabrina. "But I appreciate your help. You seem to be the only one who's doing *anything* to help. I hope you're right, and that the police take your new evidence seriously. For Mariann, and for those other girls as well."

And then, without another word, Lupe stood and went back to work, leaving Sabrina to bear the heavy weight of responsibility for whatever came next.

CHAPTER TWENTY-EIGHT

After Lupe went back to work, Sabrina hopped on her bike and pedaled the few miles to the police station. As she rode she tried to make sense of all the things she'd learned over the past week. So far, the one thing she knew for certain was that Asher Grey seemed to be in all the wrong places at exactly the right time.

Sabrina chained her bike to a phone pole in front of the police station and made her way inside. The desk officer saw her and waved her on back. "He's at his desk. I'll let him know you're here."

Sabrina waved and waited for the officer to buzz her through to the detectives' area. Once inside she wove through the labyrinth of desks to where her uncle sat. He looked up when she walked over and grinned.

"Hey there, kiddo. I've been meaning to call you—"

Sabrina cut him off and slid the report she'd typed up that afternoon across the desk. "I've been investigating Scream Site more since I saw you last, and I think I have better evidence this time. I was able to tie another missing girl to Scream Site and Shady99 and—"

"Slow down, slow down. Take a breath." He frowned and picked up the paperwork.

Sabrina followed his orders and took a deep breath, then let it out. "I really think Scream Site is why these girls have gone missing. I pulled a list of all the missing girls in a sixty-mile radius and then tried to cross reference it with the website. I managed to find one other girl besides Mariann who disappeared in a very similar way. You can see that both of the girls had number one videos of the day on Scream Site. And it looks like they were both filmed at Funland. I think Cicely might have been threatened by Shady99 too, but I don't have her login info, so I can't see if Shady messaged her. But her videos stopped after January."

Sabrina lapsed into silence as her uncle studied the report she'd typed up, his forehead furrowed as he read. "What about the other two girls?"

Sabrina bit her lip. "I couldn't find anything for them—yet. I couldn't find out if they had accounts. Both Mariann and Cicely Jones had pictures on their billboards that I was able to find, and videos that hit the number one daily spot shortly before they went missing."

Sabrina watched as her uncle put her meticulously gathered report down and gave her a patient smile. "OK, I'll check into this. But tell me, how are *you* doing kiddo? Your mom said you were working on an application for an internship over at the *Daily Sun*. I know the editor there—do you need a letter of recommendation or anything?"

Sabrina took a small step back, taken aback by her uncle's sudden changing of the topic. "No, I'll be fine. But, what about my report? You aren't going to try to get the Internet user records or anything?"

Uncle John sighed and leaned back in his chair. "That would require a subpoena, and that requires a judge thinking that there is merit to this idea. I'm afraid that what you have here, Sabrina, is likely a coincidence. There's nothing tying these two girls together except a website that millions of teens use. I appreciate that you're trying to help, but chasing down shadows like this isn't going to bring him back."

Frustration brought hot tears to Sabrina's eyes, and she blinked hard to chase them away. "I know what I saw, Uncle John. . . . Wait—*him*?"

"Your dad, Sabrina," he said quietly.

Sabrina shook her head in confusion. "This isn't about my dad. . . . "

"You're going through a tough time, and I hate to see you like this."

"Uncle John, no, you've got it wrong. I'm serious about this. There are girls missing, and no one seems to care."

Uncle John smiled kindly, but Sabrina couldn't help but feel like it was more condescending than kind. "I know it might seem that way, but lots of police departments have already gone down this road, and in the end, it's just people making thriller videos. I'm sorry you got sucked into this nonsense, but you really need to let it go. It isn't healthy, and I know your mom wouldn't be happy if she knew you were out there trying to catch kidnappers and the like. Go home and watch some TV, veg out, and forget about this before someone gets hurt."

"That's the problem, Uncle John," Sabrina said, trying to keep the anger out of her voice. "Someone already is getting hurt—the girls in those videos. Or at least they might be. And the longer everyone believes the videos are fake, the longer the person responsible will keep hurting them."

Before he could say another word, and before she could embarrass herself by bawling like a little kid, Sabrina ran out of the police station.

CHAPTER TWENTY-NINE

Sabrina pedaled home from the police station slowly, her body aching with disappointment. She'd worked so hard to tie all the clues together, but no one would listen to her. All her hard work and Uncle John still said the same thing: It was just a huge coincidence.

But it didn't feel like a coincidence, and if she heard that word one more time, she thought she might lose it. She believed Scream Site was a place where bad things happened. Really bad things.

But if Uncle John didn't take Sabrina seriously,

where did that leave Mariann Sanchez and the others? Mariann could still be alive. Maybe she was out there right now, praying and hoping for someone to come and save her. How could Sabrina give up on her? If it were *her* sister, Sabrina would want someone to try everything possible before they gave up.

Lupe was right. Whatever came next in the case would be because of Sabrina. Uncle John clearly wasn't interested in her evidence, and after their earlier conversation, Sabrina got the feeling that Lupe was starting to lose hope. Sabrina had to keep working the case. She couldn't just let Lupe down like that.

She wouldn't.

Sabrina was so wrapped up in the merry-go-round of her thoughts that she didn't notice the car following her at first. It wasn't quite dark out yet, but the sky was starting to slide toward the pinks and purples of sunset. She had no trouble seeing as she pedaled down the familiar streets of Port Riverton, which was why the car behind seemed strange. Its headlights were on, and not the normal headlights that people kept on all the time. These were bright, like high beams. They hit her like a spotlight, and she had to shield her eyes as she looked back at the car creeping up on her.

She could avoid the annoying car if she took a different route. So instead of going the regular way home, Sabrina turned off onto the rural road that bordered Port Riverton. It was a longer way to get home, but much less traveled. She wouldn't have to worry about pushy drivers there.

The car behind her fell back and Sabrina sighed in relief. She kept pedaling, letting the rhythm of her legs erase the irritation and frustration of the day. She could still prove that Shady99 was connected to the missing girls. She just had to find another angle. What was the one thing that connected all of them? She had a feeling she knew what it was, but the pieces just hadn't clicked yet.

Headlights flashed at Sabrina, and she turned around. The car was behind her again. That was weird. Hadn't the car kept going straight when she'd turned? But it was definitely the same car. The lights were still too bright, the beams on high.

There wasn't any other traffic around.

Sabrina was well to the right of the painted shoulder line, just like her dad had always told her. "Don't ever assume you have the right of way," he'd said. "If you go up against a car, you can be right or you can be alive." Sabrina always yielded to drivers. It was just safer that way.

There wasn't much space for her to move over. In this part of town, there weren't any sidewalks, just a narrow gravel shoulder between the ditch and the road. Sabrina guided her bike as closely as she could to the edge. Maybe the car would just go around. "Jerk," she muttered. She balanced her tires carefully over the large rocks she was being forced to ride on near the ditch.

But the car kept following, slowing down to a pace that was way below the speed limit. A sick feeling came over Sabrina, like her stomach was filled with worms, and she pulled all the way over to the ditch. The car behind her could now easily drive past her and go about its business.

But instead of pulling around Sabrina, the car stopped, the engine idling, the driver hidden behind the too-bright headlights.

The worms turned into icy claws of fear in her stomach. This wasn't a random driver trying to get around her.

This was someone trying to send her a message. And whatever it was, it wasn't good.

Sabrina started up again, pedaling faster, trying to stay close to the edge, rocks shifting under her tires as she went and causing the bike to wobble. Behind her, the car kept pace.

Whoever they were, they wanted to scare Sabrina. It was working. She pedaled as hard as she could, but there was no way she could outrun a car. Sabrina wanted to believe that the car was following her for a harmless reason, but she couldn't think of what that would be. Evelyn's warning came back to her: "What happens if the person you're investigating finds out?" This had to be related to Scream Site and to Shady99. There was no other reason for someone to be after her.

Which meant that she was in real danger.

Sabrina forced her legs to move as fast as they could, her brain racing just like her bike. She had to do something. She didn't know who this person was, and it was at least ten minutes to her house. She couldn't pull out her phone and dial 911, not while she was pedaling this hard. And if she stopped, who knew what would happen? They were on an old country road that went past nothing but farms. Sabrina liked to come out this way whenever she was upset, but tonight it had been a mistake. Now she was in the middle of nowhere with a stranger on her tail and no chance to call for help.

Sabrina started to slow down. Her legs felt like mush, and it was no use anyway. No matter how fast she went, the car could always go faster.

Sabrina rode past the sign for Gunderson's Farm store, and a little of her fear dissipated as a plan began to form. Gunderson's was a seasonal produce stand that was also a pumpkin patch in the fall. She didn't think it was open at this time of year, since it was still too early for spring vegetables. But the Gundersons lived on the farm as well as ran their business from it.

They might be home. Getting there and getting help might be her only chance.

Sabrina turned right down the dirt road that led to the farm store. Behind her the car hesitated for a moment, and then she heard the engine accelerate.

"Help!" Sabrina yelled. She had a moment to turn around and see the headlights barreling down on her before she swerved her bike into the ditch, going end over end. There was a moment of weightlessness, and Sabrina sent out a quick prayer that the landing wouldn't be too hard.

She slammed into the soft grasses at the bottom of the ditch, her bike flying off to the side. Sabrina lay on the ground, dazed, the car lights shining into her eyes. Her heart pounded as she waited in terror for the driver to get out of the car.

But the vehicle backed up, turned around, and sped off in a cloud of dust.

CHAPTER THIRTY

"Are you sure you're all right?" Mrs. Sebastian asked for the millionth time.

"I'm fine, Mom," Sabrina said, wincing as she adjusted in her seat, trying to get more comfortable. Everything hurt, but there was no way she could tell her mom that. Next thing she knew she'd be at the emergency room, getting a million X-rays. She hadn't even told her how she'd ended up in the ditch. Instead, Sabrina had given her mother a fake story about having a flat tire and turning off the main road to check it, only to lose control and fall down the small slope alongside the road. Her lying skills seemed to be improving. She knew if she did tell her mom the truth, that would be the end of everything, and Sabrina's fear from the incident was morphing into anger and determination. No way was she letting some creep scare her off.

But still, a dull thrum of anxiety had settled into Sabrina's middle. Mostly, she just felt irritated that she had panicked. She should've been smarter. Written down the license plate, gotten the make and model of the car, something. It didn't matter that the high beams had blinded her and her first good look at the car had been when it drove off through the gravel dust, obscuring all the details. She should have kept her wits about her and paid better attention. But she'd been too scared, and in her panic, she'd gotten nothing but a bunch of bruises and scrapes.

And a bike that was utterly destroyed.

"We can drop your bike at the shop later this week. I think they're probably closed for the day now," Sabrina's mom said, completely oblivious to Sabrina's emotional upheaval.

Sabrina nodded, but her ruined bike was the least of her concerns.

There was no doubt that the person driving that car had to somehow be related to Shady99. Who else could want her hurt? Sabrina didn't have any enemies. Not even kids that she didn't really like. Sabrina hadn't gone out or done much, especially after Mr. Sebastian died. Could it be someone who was mad at either her dad or uncle? They were cops, and cops sometimes had enemies. But that seemed too random, especially with the timing. It couldn't be a coincidence that all this had happened after she'd taken her evidence to Uncle John.

But how did somebody find that out? Did Shady99 somehow know what Sabrina had uncovered about Scream Site and the missing girls? It wasn't like she'd messaged them. In fact, Sabrina had been too afraid to, because it seemed like a pretty terrible idea to message someone and accuse them of kidnapping. She'd considered sending Shady99 a message dozens of times but each time had talked herself out of what was obviously a bad idea born out of desperation. So, there was no way that Shady99 would know she even existed.

Her mind scrambled to think of who else knew anything. The only people she'd told about her suspicions were Evelyn and Mrs. Wembley. Evelyn wasn't great at keeping a secret, so it was entirely plausible that she'd let something slip to someone, and then Asher might have found out everything Sabrina suspected. And, while Asher had said he thought he was being framed, maybe that was just the story he was going with. He could've just said that to throw

Sabrina—and the police—off track. Could he really be Shady99? He was old enough to drive a car, but she didn't know if he had a license.

If it wasn't Asher, that left only Wembley who knew anything. It was ridiculous to think of Mrs. Wembley being Shady99. She didn't even like the Internet. Why would she kidnap girls to make videos and post them? The person who was taking those girls had to have a reason for it, even if the reason was just a chance to get famous.

While Sabrina was racking her brain, it occurred to her that Faith also knew about Sabrina's investigation. But since she never took her seriously, Faith probably wasn't the leak in her case. Unless maybe she'd blabbed to her friends about what a gullible kid her little sister was, trying to play detective. . . .

That was everyone she could think of who knew anything. But then Sabrina's brain ground to a halt. That wasn't right. There *were* more people who knew about Scream Site and her investigation. There was Lupe. Could she be telling Shady everything Sabrina was doing? Were Lupe and Mariann and Shady all working together? *Was Lupe Shady?* Sabrina quickly dismissed that crazy idea. Because there was no way Lupe would be trying to get the police involved if she was the bad buy.

And then, there was Uncle John. He knew what she

was up to, as well. But he certainly hadn't been the one behind the wheel of that car. That was impossible—that Uncle John could be someone who would kidnap girls or threaten to hurt his own niece in any way. She felt bad for even thinking about him being Shady99. She was clearly losing her grip on reality.

But what if Shady99 was someone who worked in the police station? That might explain why the disappearances weren't being taken seriously. If there was a police officer in the station making sure that the investigations into the Scream Site connection never went anywhere, then Shady99 could keep doing whatever they liked and hurting whoever they wanted.

No matter who had been behind the wheel, that car meant that Sabrina was on the right track with her investigation. It meant that whoever Shady99 was, it was someone Sabrina knew, or at least someone who knew her. Whoever was behind the wheel in that car had wanted to harm Sabrina. That was something Sabrina couldn't forget. Not now, not ever.

The more she thought about it, the angrier she got, thinking about some jerk trying to scare her, to hurt her, to intimidate her into quitting, or worse. Because while all of her family and friends wanted her to leave the whole Scream Site case alone, now she was more certain than ever that she was on to something. And that meant she had to keep going.

Sabrina startled as her mother pulled into the driveway. She been so involved in her mental gymnastics that she'd barely noticed the drive.

"Make sure you jump into a warm shower and wash off those scrapes," her mom said as they got out of the car. "The warm water should also ease any aches. I'll make dinner while you get cleaned up, sweetheart."

"OK," said Sabrina, walking gingerly. She followed her mother into the house and headed upstairs.

After a quick shower Sabrina felt much better. The warm water did ease her tense muscles and washed away some of the residual fear. Now she could think more clearly. And she was ready to work.

Sabrina opened her laptop. Maybe she could try something new to tie the girls to Shady99. She had just logged in when a message popped up on her screen. She clicked it open, and her breath hitched in her chest.

The message was from Shady99 and there was only a single line of unpunctuated text:

next time i wont miss

CHAPTER THIRTY-ONE

Sabrina didn't sleep at all that night. When she lay down in her bed and closed her eyes, all she saw were those two bright headlights barreling down on her. Sometimes she dreamed it was Asher driving; other times it was one of the missing girls, screaming for help. No matter the dream, the end result was the same: Sabrina bolted awake, heart pounding, chest tight with fear.

School the next day wasn't much better. Somehow it had gotten around school that Sabrina thought Asher was maybe a psycho killer/kidnapper and had called the police on him. People were now giving

Sabrina a wide berth, and even Evelyn was skeptical.

"Look, Sabrina, I told you this was a bad idea," she said after school as they sat in Lou's Brews. Nearby a table of popular girls shot Sabrina pointed glances while they whispered. She tried to ignore it, but it was impossible. Being the subject of gossip was no fun.

Evelyn pretended to be oblivious to the whole thing, although she did throw a piece of muffin in the girls' direction when they weren't looking. "Maybe you should just let it go," she said.

Sabrina groaned. She hadn't told Evelyn about the car on the back road because she knew that she'd freak out. For all Evelyn's daring, she was pretty much all talk.

"I can't let it go, Ev. I really want to find this guy and make sure he ends up behind bars. Besides, I can't just give up on Mariann Sanchez. And what about the other girls? They might still be alive."

"Do you really think someone is kidnapping girls and making videos without the police finding out? I know Lupe thinks the police are incompetent, but you know your uncle. There's no way he would let something bad happen to someone without stepping in if he could. I mean, he won't even let me skateboard in the park." Evelyn made a face and shook her head. "It just doesn't make sense. Even if they did go missing because of the website, they're probably dead. There's nothing you can do."

Sabrina shot Evelyn a scolding look about the callous comment. "I can't give up hope. I'm close. I know it. I just need to know how Shady got to them."

Evelyn took a long drink of her usual chai with extra whipped cream. Sabrina had ordered an extra-large mocha with double shots of espresso. It felt like it had been forever since she'd had a good night's sleep, and her eyes felt gritty and hot. The Scream Site investigation was really taking its toll. She was behind on all her homework, and she hadn't even started writing her article for the school newspaper or finished her application for the internship. Everything was falling apart, and still Sabrina had a driving need to keep digging, to figure out the truth behind Scream Site and Mariann and the others.

Evelyn watched her with a critical eye, lips pursed. "Well, you have to do something, because you look terrible and I know you got a B on the last biology test."

Sabrina sighed. "One B isn't *that* bad."

"Not for me, maybe. But it is for you, Ms. Four-Point-Oh. And now everyone is talking about you at school like you've lost your mind. If this keeps up, you're going to be unpopular *and* have bad grades. That's a recipe for sadness."

"You know I don't care about popularity," Sabrina

said, trying to change the subject.

"I do!" Evelyn exclaimed loud enough that the lady at the next table looked over in surprise. Evelyn ducked her head and lowered her voice "I care about popularity, and I need you to pull it together, Sabrina. We are perfectly positioned to be in the mid-tier of cool next year, which means we will at least be popular enough to get invited to the good parties. But that's not going to happen if you keep up with running around like this. You need a plan."

Sabrina sighed and threw her hands into the air. "What kind of plan?"

Before Evelyn could explain, Faith hurried over, her brown skin flushed, a wide grin on her face, and her phone in hand. "You guys, guess what?" Her sleek bob was still perfectly smooth, even though the front was a bit mussed, like she had been jumping up and down or something.

"As soon as we finish our drinks we'll head out," Sabrina said, remembering how Faith hated when they hung out for too long.

"Oh, no, you're fine. I just wanted to show you this. Look, my video is *number one* on Scream Site," Faith said, bouncing on her toes and solving the mystery of her slightly messy hair.

"What? That's awesome," Evelyn said, jumping up to see Faith's phone. Sabrina stayed where she was, her mocha stalled halfway to her lips. Dread chilled her despite the coffee's warmth.

Faith turned to show her sister the phone, and Sabrina forced a smile. "Wow, that's great," Sabrina said as her sister grinned. "I know you worked really hard on that video."

"I know. This is so exciting. I have to figure out what I'm going to do next. You know, I have to start thinking about college, and this makes me think that film school really could be a possibility. This could be my big break! Oh, there's Asher. I have to tell him."

"Asher?" Sabrina said, alarm bells clanging loudly in her mind. She craned her neck toward the front door where Asher was entering with a group of boys from the baseball team.

"Of course! He's a huge fan of Scream Site. He was the one who got me into it in the first place. Talk to you guys later."

Faith skipped across the restaurant in delight, holding her phone up so that the group of boys congregating in the entryway could see. They cheered and high-fived Faith, celebrating with her like Sabrina should have been but couldn't. Sabrina watched Asher's face, to see if he would show any anger over Faith taking the top spot. After all, Shady99 would be livid to lose that ranking.

But Asher just looked happy for his friend.

"OK, what's going on? Why do you look like someone stole your cat all of a sudden?" Evelyn asked.

"Both Mariann Sanchez and Cicely Jones had number one videos before they went missing," Sabrina said, frowning. "And Asher told me he wasn't on Scream Site when I talked to him."

"So?"

"So, he lied. Faith just said that Asher was the one who told her about the website in the first place. What else is he lying about?"

Evelyn followed Sabrina's gaze to where Faith laughed with the boys. "So what? What does all that mean?"

"I think it means that Asher knows more than he's saying. And if he does, I need to find out what it is. I have to figure out who is behind the Shady99 account, before Faith is the next victim."

Evelyn quirked an eyebrow. "Do you really think the Scream Site dude is going to kidnap your sister?"

"I don't know. I'm pretty sure that Shady99 is local," Sabrina said, trailing off before she said too much. She watched Asher talking to Faith. Concern filled her with dread and settled like a stone in her belly. Once again she had the urge to tell Evelyn about the car, and the ditch, and the very real fear that maybe Asher was behind the entire mess, even though he denied it. But Sabrina didn't. She was tired of people thinking she was foolish.

She wasn't going to make that mistake again. She'd keep things to herself, since no one believed her anyway.

Evelyn took a long drink of her chai. "Well, then, I guess we have some work to do," she said, dragging Sabrina back to the conversation. "Let's go figure out just where Shady99 is located."

CHAPTER
THIRTY-TWO

Evelyn had the idea to go to the library to research instead of going back to Sabrina's house.

"Look, you've obviously watched this Shady99 guy's videos like a ton of times. Maybe we should log in from a different location, just to cover our tracks. Plus, the library is right there, and I don't feel like walking all the way to your house," Evelyn said, matter-of-factly.

It seemed as good an idea as any, and it wasn't like Sabrina had any others. At this point she was just a bundle of anxiety and nerves, and it had taken everything she had not to run over to Asher and shove him away from her sister. Seeing Faith so happy to tell him the news about her video when Sabrina knew Asher could be dangerous made her feel helpless and small.

The most important thing she had to do now was figure out who Shady99 really was. And maybe if she found compelling enough evidence, she could try one more time to get Uncle John involved. But not until then. She couldn't have him look at her with pity again.

Evelyn and Sabrina signed into a computer in the back of the reference area, stowing their backpacks under the desk. Evelyn sat at the keyboard and logged into her own Scream Site account.

"You could've logged into mine," Sabrina said.

"If someone is tracking your account, then you need to snoop using a different one," Evelyn said. "Mine is a totally unknown entity."

"What are you planning?" Sabrina asked, watching Evelyn type.

"Remember when I told you I had a plan?" Ev asked. "Well, Scream Site has a feature where you can message a user directly. I think I could probably do a reverse IP look up on the instant messenger of Shady99, if they agree to talk to me. That way, you'd at least know if they're anywhere in the area."

Sabrina pulled a chair over and sank into it.

"That's actually a great idea. How did you learn to do that?"

Evelyn snorted. "Hello? Hacker U, remember?"

"Oh yeah, right," Sabrina said. "Your criminal training camp."

"Yeah, I knew this would come in handy. And look, here we are." Evelyn sent a direct message to Shady99. It was simple: "omg, luv your videos."

Evelyn leaned back in the chair. "And now we wait."

Sabrina sighed. "I hate this. Faith could be in danger and we're sitting here sending fan mail to the enemy."

Evelyn shrugged and clicked on one of Shady99's videos. "You know, all of these kind of look familiar."

"That's because I showed them to you."

"No, I mean I know I've seen them somewhere else before. Maybe a movie or something?" Evelyn frowned. "Anyway, I don't think your boy Shady is creating his own content. I think he's copying something else."

Shady99's video, the one with a girl wearing red ballet flats, began to play. It was one of the videos Sabrina had skipped after only a few minutes because it was too creepy. In it the girl was being chased through what seemed to be a mirror maze, her feet the only thing visible as she tried to flee. Without the sound it just seemed cheesy, but with the sound on, it had been terrifying. The girl's crying, the screaming, the begging to please be let go. It was strange how different things could look from a new perspective.

The screen blinked, and Evelyn gave a happy squeal. "Here we go!"

She closed the window and opened another, typing so fast that Sabrina could only register Shady99's response:

Thanx. New vid up later.

"Wait, he's going to have a new video up later," Sabrina said, while Evelyn right clicked, scrolled through the source code, and opened another window.

"Cool, let's hope he doesn't—crap."

"Wait, what happened?" Sabrina asked.

"He disconnected from the chat. Doesn't matter, I was able to pull his IP address. Hopefully we can reverse search—huh?"

"What?" Sabrina asked, peering at the computer screen.

"Well, it turns out Shady99 really is a Port Riverton local. You were right, Sabrina." Evelyn's shoulders drooped.

Sabrina shrugged. "So, I was right. Why do you look like you've seen a ghost?"

"Because the address that came back was Port Riverton High School."

Sabrina stared at Evelyn in surprise. "Does that mean what I think it does?"

Evelyn nodded. "I think you're right. Asher really might be Shady99."

CHAPTER THIRTY-THREE

By the time Sabrina got home, she was exhausted and out of sorts. She and Evelyn had watched every single one of Shady99's videos, twice. There was nothing to tie Asher to the videos directly, and there was still no way of figuring out what the girls in the videos looked like, since their faces were mostly obscured no matter how many times they paused the playback.

Sabrina didn't want to go to her Uncle John again. He already thought that she was making herself crazy with what he seemed to consider her grief-induced obsession about the disappearance of Mariann Sanchez. If she gave him this latest piece of information—that they'd pinned Shady's IP account to her own high school—he would probably have her mom cut off her Internet privileges for a week.

And besides, no one was going to believe that sweet, kind, cute Asher Grey was a kidnapper who tormented his captives on camera for clicks. Sabrina wasn't sure she could believe it herself. It just didn't make any kind of sense.

Sabrina didn't know what to make of the fact that Shady99's IP routed back to the school. Even though it seemed like that could be the evidence she needed to link Asher to Scream Site, there was a tiny problem: There was no way he could be uploading the videos or messaging at school. Sabrina herself had tried to use Scream Site there, but it was blocked. So how was Shady using it from there if she couldn't? Had they somehow gotten through the fire wall?

Plus, they'd seen Asher at Lou's Brews not long before messaging Shady99. He couldn't be in two places at once. It was possible he'd gone back to school after picking something up at Lou's, but Sabrina didn't think so. Asher could be working with someone else, but who? And why would they be using the high school's Internet? Was it some other student who had broken through the fire wall somehow? Or were they using staff login credentials that bypassed the fire wall?

All of it was very upsetting, and with the added worry about Faith getting mixed up in it, Sabrina was completely at her wit's end. What was she supposed to do with all this when it just seemed to keep getting more and more confusing? Not only that, but she still had to get her application for the internship done— the thing that had sent her down this insane rabbit hole in the first place. The Scream Site investigation had taken over her whole life.

Sabrina walked into the house, exhausted. She truly didn't know what to do or where to turn next.

That was when Sabrina's phone pinged. She had a new notification from Scream Site.

Recently Sabrina had downloaded the app and set it to alert her whenever certain users posted: Mariann's old account, Shady99, and the couple of accounts she'd thought might belong to the missing girls. Her most recent add had been Faith's account, just to keep an eye on her sister. The app was also set up to alert her to any new messages that came to her account, not that she got many.

Sabrina clicked on the Scream Site logo to check this latest notification. It was a message to her from an account she didn't recognize. The message was simple:

Horror99: I see you

There was a file attached. Sabrina hit the preview button on the image, in case it was some kind of phishing attempt. Faith had clicked on files in an email last year and had allowed a scammer to steal all her information—her passwords, her account usernames, everything—leaving behind a nasty virus that had locked up her phone. It was before Mr. Sebastian had died, and their parents had been so mad. The last thing Sabrina wanted was to mess up the same way.

But the preview very quickly revealed that it wasn't any kind of phishing attempt. The file was a picture.

Of Evelyn and Sabrina.

Sabrina's heart pounded in her chest. The picture showed Sabrina and Evelyn at Funland, when they had been there searching for any sign of where Mariann might have disappeared to.

Someone knew what they were up to and wanted them to stop.

CHAPTER THIRTY-FOUR

Sabrina paced back and forth in the dining room while her mom talked to Uncle John. After getting the photo, Sabrina had finally been scared enough to call her mom at work, blubbering out the entire story over the phone. This was the second warning someone had sent to her, and Sabrina was too scared to wait for a third. She knew when she was in over her head, and this was definitely too much. She needed help. So Sabrina told her mother everything, from the day she'd spoken to Lupe Sanchez to the strange car running her off the road.

Sabrina had thought she could solve this case,

she'd thought she could handle what she was getting involved in. But she couldn't. She was scared. And the way she could barely stand upright proved it.

Uncle John walked over and put a calming hand on Sabrina's arm. "It's going to be OK."

"No, it isn't," Sabrina said, tears threatening once more. She shrugged off his hands and wrapped her arms around herself. "You think I'm making this all up, that this is some kind of practical joke. But I know why this is happening. Those girls did go missing because of Scream Site, and as long Shady99 is out there, no one is safe."

Uncle John and Sabrina's mother exchanged a long look. "I should have told you this a couple weeks ago when she first came to me, but I thought it would blow over," he said to Mrs. Sebastian.

Sabrina's mother's face was wrinkled with concern. "Sabrina, why don't you go upstairs so John and I can talk? I'll come check on you in a bit."

Sabrina's anger resurfaced through her fear. "I'm not a child. And I have evidence! Someone is using Scream Site to find girls and then terrifying them in order to make scary videos. If we can figure out who Shady99 is, we can save all those girls and stop Shady before he comes for Faith. We can stop all this!"

"Sabrina, you've got to calm down!" Mrs. Sebastian said, loudly enough to make Uncle John grimace.

Sabrina froze. Her mother hadn't yelled at her like that in a very long time, and her anger melted back into shame and embarrassment.

Sabrina turned and ran up the stairs to her room, throwing herself on her bed and finally giving in to tears. For the last couple of weeks, she'd tried to get to the bottom of this mystery, and now she was so close, but no one would help her. Even Evelyn, who was usually game for any kind of challenge, thought Sabrina was in over her head. It was too dangerous, too risky. And maybe a little too far-fetched.

But Sabrina felt like she was on the right track. Didn't the car and the threatening photos prove as much? Why go to all this trouble to scare her if she wasn't really close to cracking the whole thing open?

There was a soft knock on her door before it opened a few inches. Mrs. Sebastian peeked her head around the corner. "Hey, can we talk?"

Sabrina shrugged, still too angry and upset to really answer her mom. Mrs. Sebastian didn't seem to notice, because she walked into the room and sat next to Sabrina on the bed.

"Why didn't you tell me any of this was going on?" she asked in a low voice. Her gentle words loosened the knot of Sabrina's frustration, and she sighed.

"I didn't want to bother you. I know you're really busy with your job. And I didn't know if you'd believe me, anyway. Uncle John didn't, and I figured if I just kept digging, if I solved the case, I could tell you then."

"Baby, I am never too busy for you. But what brought this on in the first place? I know you told me that you began investigating this for that internship, and I know how much you want to be a reporter. But this all seems a bit much for you. Do you think maybe this was all just because you were trying to distract yourself?"

"From what?" Sabrina asked. Her mother was going somewhere with this conversation, but even with a map and GPS, Sabrina couldn't have said where.

"From the anniversary of your dad's death."

Sabrina opened her mouth to object and then snapped it closed. A terrible feeling came over her, and her shoulders slumped. She'd forgotten all about the anniversary of her father's death. Next week it would be one year since he'd gone out for groceries and died on the way home, a massive heart attack that the doctors said had killed him instantly.

"I know how much you girls liked going to Funland with your dad—it was kind of like a tradition for you three. And Gunderson's isn't that far from where he died. The symbolism hasn't escaped me, Sabrina."

The merry-go-round of guilt ground to a halt. *Symbolism?*

"I understand why you might be imagining all these crazy things. You don't feel safe, and I'm so sorry about that, honey. I worry that you're fabricating things that aren't there, and it just breaks my heart to think of how much you're hurting." Mrs. Sebastian squeezed Sabrina's shoulder. "I'll make an appointment for us to go and talk to Dr. Shepard in a couple of days. Maybe you and Faith both quit grief counseling too soon. I don't like the way she's obsessed with this boy she met online. And you getting wrapped up in this website and missing girls. . . . " Mrs. Sebastian trailed off, shaking her head. "I'm also going to try to cut back my hours at the hospital. I thought we were doing better, but I realize now that we have a ways to go. I'm sorry I haven't been here for you as much I should have."

Mrs. Sebastian stood and gave Sabrina a kiss on the forehead before leaving the room. Sabrina didn't say anything in response to the suggestion that Sabrina had *made up* the pictures and the car that had tried to run her off the road. How did her mother think she'd gotten the picture of her and Evelyn? Did she think she'd asked Tony or someone to take it of them, and then sent it to herself? It stung that her mother thought she'd do something so juvenile as making up a fake stalker just for attention.

And then an even worse thought occurred to Sabrina. *Could there be any truth to that?*

CHAPTER
THIRTY-FIVE

Sabrina spent the next couple days not thinking about Scream Site. Well, trying not to think about Scream Site, at least. She caught up on all her homework, came home right after school each day, and generally did all the things she'd done before the missing girls and Shady99 had taken over her life.

Her mom traded a couple of her double shifts away to another nurse, so she was home for dinner every night. Even Faith took fewer hours at Lou's Brews and canceled plans with her friends so that she could be home for dinner too. It wasn't like she had much choice since Mrs. Sebastian wasn't a parent you could defy, not without losing a phone or other privileges. But it was nice to have family dinners nonetheless.

It was all so normal and nice that Sabrina had nearly convinced her family that she'd forgotten about Scream Site. But she hadn't.

Everything seemed to conspire against Sabrina and her promise to avoid Scream Site. First, there was the fact that everyone at school was excited about Faith's video being number one.

"It's like you're related to a movie star," Evelyn said at lunch one day as they watched everyone gathered around Faith and her friends' table. The video had become so popular that the school newspaper had even featured an interview with Faith about her creative process. The story had gone in the spot where Sabrina's Scream Site feature was supposed to go, because she still had yet to write the story. She'd never missed a deadline before, but the due date for her story came and went with nothing completed. And after everything that had happened, Sabrina wasn't certain she ever would get the article written. She just didn't know what the truth looked like anymore, and she had nothing concrete to report.

Which was no good for her internship application. It sat untouched on her desk at home. Sabrina finally gave in and sent in her exposé on the cafeteria's mostly meatless tacos. It seemed beyond underwhelming after her time spent investigating actual crimes. She didn't have time to write anything else, and she didn't have the heart to include the article on the charity drive since Asher was mentioned in it. She wanted to forget everything about Scream Site, including him.

That should have been the end of it, but Mrs. Wembley kept pressing Sabrina for more details on her story. She had asked Sabrina for an update, and then a new due date, to the point where Sabrina now dreaded going to English class because she knew Mrs. Wembley was going to corner her again.

"I'm still working on it but taking it in a different direction," Sabrina said when Mrs. Wembley stopped her after class one day, as predicted.

"What kind of direction?" Mrs. Wembley asked.

"Umm, I'm not sure yet," Sabrina muttered, hurrying away before Mrs. Wembley could ask anything else.

But even her own traitorous brain wouldn't stop thinking about Scream Site. In the moments during class when she was staring off into space, she'd start to think about it, to wonder who Shady99 was and how they were connected to her high school. Shady could be one of the students or teachers in the building at that very minute. Sabrina shivered.

Sabrina's thoughts turned to Asher. He had been nothing but nice to her, even after she accused him of maybe being a psycho who lured girls off the Internet. But the only evidence she had pointed to him as being the most likely candidate. His picture had been sent to Mariann, the IP address linked back to the school, he mysteriously had Sabrina's printouts about the missing girls, and he'd been acting really weird ever since this all started. Unless he was acting weird because he still hadn't told Sabrina everything he knew. She couldn't help but feel that he was hiding something.

A week to the day after promising her mother that she would stop investigating Scream Site, Sabrina cornered Asher after school at Lou's Brews. She and Evelyn were at their usual table, but the moment Asher walked in, Sabrina strode over to him, halting his progress toward the counter.

"I know there's something you still aren't telling me," Sabrina said without hesitation.

Asher's expression flickered from surprise to acceptance, and he sighed in defeat. "You're right," he said, surprising Sabrina.

"So, what is it?" Sabrina asked, crossing her arms and trying to feel tough, like a hardboiled detective. She mostly felt silly—but also a little excited. Maybe this was finally the piece of information that would fit all the pieces of the puzzle together.

Asher took a deep breath and let it out. "I went

back and rewatched the videos on Shady99's billboard. And I think I know who might be involved."

Hope leapt in Sabrina's chest. "What? Who? You have to tell me!"

Asher shook his head. "I shouldn't say."

Sabrina grabbed Asher by the arm and dragged him out of the line. He seemed startled. Poor guy really was on edge. Sabrina made a split-second decision based on instinct. She would have to believe that Asher wasn't actually Shady99, that he was just a guy in the wrong place at the wrong time. She decided to tell him what she knew, and maybe they could work together.

"Look, someone took some super creepy pictures of me and Evelyn and also tried to run me off the road, not to mention sent threatening messages to my Scream Site account. I'm freaked out and I have to figure out who this person is before Faith is next."

Asher frowned. "Faith? What's she got to do with this?"

"Two of the girls who disappeared in this area had number one videos on Scream Site, knocking Shady99 out of the top spot. Now Faith has one."

"But what about girls in other areas? There are lots of videos that get to be the daily video."

"I know. That's why I think there has to be something else that connects them, not just the number one video thing. Something local. You have to tell me what you know."

Asher sighed and ran his hand through his hair. "Well, I can tell you that every single one of those girls in the videos was wearing a Funland uniform," he said in a low voice, looking around to make sure they weren't being overheard.

"How do you know that?"

"Like I told you, I worked there for a little while last summer. It was the worst. The owner, Dan, didn't pay us on time and the work was gross. Do you know what happens in those bathrooms?" Asher gave a shudder, like someone had walked over his grave. "Anyway, if you're still checking it out, look into Dan Mason. That dude was weird. He had like six dogs in a kennel in the back and was always talking about how he'd be rich if only the movie had happened."

Sabrina nodded as she digested this piece of information. "What movie? And wait—why were you so freaked out to tell me this?"

"Because I've been getting messages as well," Asher said. "And I'm scared too. But keep this to yourself, OK? Promise me you won't tell anyone."

Sabrina nodded. "Promise."

"Something super weird is happening here. I just want it to end." When someone called his name, Asher tipped his chin at Sabrina, then went to join his friend.

Sabrina was already thinking about how to research Funland. Lupe Sanchez had said that a bunch of Scream Site kids used Funland as a shooting location. Mariann Sanchez was supposed to meet someone at Funland when she went missing. And now Asher said the uniforms the girls were wearing were from Funland. Everything kept coming back to that creepy, abandoned amusement park.

She was so excited about following this lead that she almost didn't feel guilty about breaking a promise to her mother.

CHAPTER THIRTY-SIX

"So what was that about?" Evelyn asked when Sabrina returned to their table after talking with Asher.

"Oh, nothing, I was just apologizing. You know, for thinking maybe he'd been a psycho killer and all," Sabrina said, remembering that she had promised Asher that she wouldn't say anything about what he'd told her.

Evelyn relaxed. "Oh, good. I didn't want to say anything, but I'm glad you're letting this all go."

Sabrina sighed. "I know."

"Honestly, it was getting kind of intense. I mean, that picture of us? That's just weird. Whoever this person is, the police will find him. It just isn't safe for you to keep digging."

Sabrina tried not to bristle. The police weren't going to find Shady99 because the police didn't even seem to be looking for him . . . or her? She hadn't told Evelyn that Uncle John and her mom seemed to think she was having some kind of hallucinations or delusions due to her grieving, and that they weren't taking the creepy photo seriously. Everyone thought she was crazy. But even Asher was scared, now. Getting threats will do that to you. And what about Faith? As far as Sabrina knew, Shady99 was even now trying to figure out how to get to her sister.

She kept her thoughts to herself, though. And if she was a bit distracted while they finished their homework and shared a giant muffin, Evelyn didn't seem to notice.

Once Sabrina got home, she ate dinner and laughed and joked, even though she was thinking about Scream Site the whole time. She excused herself after dinner and went upstairs to do homework, leaving her door open so that when Mrs. Sebastian stopped by to tell her good night, it would be obvious that she was working on a report for biology, and not researching Scream Site.

But once her mother had gone to bed, Sabrina went to her browser and typed in *Funland*. She wanted to see every single piece of news related to it.

There wasn't much. The park had opened up in the late 1970s and featured go-karts, an arcade, and mini-golf—all stuff she and Faith had done with their dad over the years. She found a cached version of Funland's website, but none of the links were working anymore. Her search also turned up web pages with expired coupons for Funland and outdated photo ads of people staged to look like they were thrilled to be there and eating junk food from the concession stand. She wondered if the owner had taken those photos himself and directed the people like actors in a play.

Sabrina thought of the last time she'd been to Funland. Evelyn had dragged her there last summer, and even then the park had looked rundown and old, like no one had thought to repaint anything. In the pictures she could find, it was easy to see that the place had been a bit ramshackle for a long time: The windmill on the mini-golf course listed to one side, the arcade games all looked like they were decades old, and the go-karts were dented and paint-chipped.

Funland didn't look like a whole lot of fun anymore. No wonder it had gone out of business.

Sabrina sighed and sat back in her chair, stifling a yawn. What had Asher said the owner's name was? Dave? No, Dan. Sabrina tried searching for Dan and Funland but came up with nothing helpful.

But Asher had also said that Dan was always going on and on about a movie or something. What was that about?

Sabrina did a new search for Funland and movie. That search was the first one that returned something useful. Sabrina clicked on a local newspaper article.

Horror Movie to Be Set in Funland

When the Scarapelli Brothers first called Daniel Mason, owner of Funland Amusement Center in Port Riverton, Mason wasn't quite sure what to think.

"It seemed like a joke, you know? These big movie producers wanting to use my little park for a horror movie. But it was for real," Mason said.

Next month the Scarapelli Brothers will start filming their latest movie, *Big Fun*, at the local arcade and fun center. The movie, which features a park operator who kidnaps teens after they visit the park, promises to be a real scream.

But Mason wouldn't know about that. "I don't like scary movies," he says, with a laugh. "They give me nightmares."

Sabrina stopped cold. Didn't the description of that movie sound an awful lot like what Sabrina thought was happening right now in real life? She skimmed the rest of the article, which was just more of Dan Mason talking about how excited he was for the opportunity and the business it might bring to his park. She went back to her search to see if there were any other articles. The only thing she found was a small clipping from a movie magazine announcing that production on the movie had been halted, but the report didn't provide any reasons why.

Sabrina rubbed her sore neck. What had happened to the movie to cause it to be canceled?

She didn't know, but she knew who would: Dan Mason.

CHAPTER THIRTY-SEVEN

After school Sabrina walked home and considered her options. She had to talk to Dan Mason, and that meant getting out to Funland. But without a bike it would be a long walk, and most of it was through farmland, where there wouldn't be anyone else around. After the creepy stalker photo and the incident with the driver, Sabrina definitely wasn't willing to take the risk.

She had tried asking Evelyn, but no luck. "It's Friday, and Tony is taking some girl out," she said. "But we could maybe try to go tomorrow."

Sabrina had nodded, but she was too impatient to wait until then. She had a feeling that talking to Dan Mason would provide the missing link, and she was desperate to figure out exactly who Shady99 was.

But if Dan Mason *was* Shady99, talking to him could be dangerous. So Sabrina was back to where she kept finding herself: stuck.

Detective work was like repeatedly hitting her head against the wall.

She walked into the house and dropped her school bag by the door. "I'm home!" she called out. Silence greeted her, as usual. Mrs. Sebastian was back on evening hours tonight, and Faith was most likely at Lou's Brews, working. It was just her, all by herself.

Sabrina's phone pinged the ringtone she'd set for incoming Scream Site notifications. She dug it out of her pocket and opened the app. Her heart began to pound as she read the alert.

Shady99 had just posted a new video.

Sabrina clicked on the link and a video began to play. Like so many others, this one featured a girl wearing the uniform that she now recognized as being from Funland—the blue collared shirt with darker blue trim. This time the girl was strapped to a chair, wiggling to get free. Her screams were muffled; Sabrina assumed there must be something covering her mouth. Like most of the other girls in recent videos, this girl could only be seen from the neck to the knees. But there was something different about this one. It definitely wasn't Mariann Sanchez. This girl's skin was a darker brown. Her neck was thinner. Then Sabrina saw the silver necklace glistening there.

She clapped her hand over her mouth. Her stomach filled with icy fear as she watched. She knew this girl. She ate dinner with her and fought with her. She'd spent every Christmas and Thanksgiving with her. It was happening again, and Sabrina hadn't been able to stop it.

And this time it was happening to Faith.

A light-headed wooziness overcame Sabrina. She wanted to stop the video, illogically thinking that if she stopped the clip, her sister would somehow stop being hurt. But she couldn't stop the video, and the begging and screaming just kept going.

"Maybe it isn't her," she whispered. "Maybe I'm just imagining it."

The camera panned out farther and Sabrina gasped out loud. The girl's shoes came into view. She recognized those shoes—the green laces, the designs along the side. Faith had been so proud when she bought them.

Sabrina's sister was the girl in video this time. There was no denying that. And it was up to Sabrina to save her.

CHAPTER THIRTY-EIGHT

Sabrina fumbled to pause the video. She had to think. She couldn't panic, because if she did, she'd be useless. She had to act calmly and logically. *Think, Sabrina, think*, she silently admonished herself. *Where is Faith supposed to be right now?*

Sabrina pulled out her phone and dialed Lou's Brews with a shaky hand. *Please, please, please let Faith be at work*, she thought. *Please don't let it be Faith in that video.* But the girl who answered at Lou's told her that Faith wasn't there.

"Is this Sabrina?" the girl asked.

"Yes. Faith always works on Fridays," Sabrina said, hoping to make it true by saying it.

The girl on the other end sighed. "She usually does, but she asked for it off today, which is why I'm here. She said she was going on a date with some guy she met."

"OK," Sabrina said, barely above a whisper, but the girl had already hung up. Panic sent a trickle of sweat down her brow, but she swiped it away. She had to find out where Faith had gone.

She tried calling Faith's cell, but it rang and rang before going to voicemail. She didn't bother leaving a message, just ended the call and then called it right back. It was their family's sign that something was seriously bad, that everything needed to stop and the phone call be answered. The last time they'd used it was after their Dad's heart attack.

This time it rang just once and then went to voicemail. Whoever had Faith's phone, whether it was her or someone else, had decided to ignore Sabrina's call.

That pushed her alarm into full blown terror.

Sabrina ran upstairs and opened the door to her sister's room. It felt strange to be in her space, since she never went in there uninvited. The room was the opposite of Sabrina's: absolute chaos. Piles of clothes dotted the carpet and her desk was covered with notes to herself. There were books and magazines strewn all over the floor, and the closet was so full that the contents spewed out onto the carpet.

Sabrina searched for Faith's laptop, carelessly turning over magazines and moving coffee cups to the side. Somewhere in the middle of her search, she started to cry, her fear for her sister too much for her body to contain. She knew that the only way she would be able to save her sister would be to figure out who she'd spoken to last. The laptop wasn't on her desk or her bed, but she finally found it by following the power cord from the wall to the space under her bed.

Sabrina reached for it and wiped her eyes and runny nose with the back of her hand as she opened it up. *Pull it together*, she ordered herself.

Faith hadn't logged out of any of her accounts, and Sabrina was able to easily pull up her email and Scream Site account. There were messages on her billboard, just like on Mariann Sanchez's—a bunch of guys telling her how much they liked her video and asking if they could send her a private message. Faith had ignored most of them except for one—a user named Scotty2Hotty.

"Oh, come on, Faith. Really?" Sabrina cried. Scotty was pretty cute, and he looked vaguely familiar.

Sabrina didn't have time to do a reverse image search, so she just clicked on Faith's private messages and scrolled through until she found the ones from Scotty. Sabrina skimmed until she found one that seemed important.

From: **Scotty2Hotty**

To: **HorrorBoyyy**

Subject: Friday?

So, since you're in Port Riverton, that is really close. We should hang out for real. You want to meet up at Funland? I've heard it's a killer spot to shoot vids, creepy and rundown.

Sabrina's breath caught. Funland. Somehow it always came back to that place.

She had to get there and find her sister.

CHAPTER THIRTY-NINE

Sabrina tried calling Evelyn but didn't get an answer, so she left a voicemail. "Hey, it's Sabrina," she said, not even trying to hide the fear in her voice. "Um, I think something's happening, and I think it's all because of this Dan Mason guy who owns Funland. I think he might be Shady99. And he might have Faith. I'm going to head out to Funland to see if I can find her. Call me."

Sabrina then tried calling her mom and Uncle John, but both of their phones went to voicemail as well. As an ER nurse, Sabrina's mom couldn't always answer her phone. It looked like Sabrina was all on her own.

She went out to the garage and stared at her bike. There was no way she could ride it. The wheels were still all bent up from her crash into the ditch and both tires were flat. Somehow they hadn't found time to get the bike to the repair shop yet.

Sabrina clearly couldn't ride her own bike, and Faith had sold hers to help pay for her car. Sabrina let out a groan of frustration and glanced around the garage. There at the very back, leaning against the wall, was her dad's old road bike. No one had touched it since he'd died. The tires were flat and the brakes squeaked a little when she tried them out, but it rolled.

Besides, she didn't have time to be choosy. Faith was in trouble.

Sabrina pumped up the tires, grabbed a helmet, and took off for Funland.

* * *

The road bike was fast, much faster than Sabrina's busted up ten-speed, and she pedaled as hard as she could, flying down the country roads toward Funland. Her heart pounded in her ears the entire trip, and not because of the exertion—because she was terrified for her sister's life.

Someone had her. That was the most likely explanation. There was no way Faith would've ignored Sabrina's call. Not after Dad. Sure, she'd been distant lately, but weren't teenagers supposed to be distant and moody? Today felt different, though. Something wasn't right.

The sign for Funland came into view, and Sabrina pedaled a little more slowly. The trees around the park were spindly, their foliage sparse with bright green leaves. She could see glimpses of the mini-golf course and the go-kart track. The arcade was housed in a cinder block building with the word FUNLAND painted on the side in an old-fashioned circus font.

The park looked empty as expected until Sabrina pulled her bike into the gravel parking lot. She saw a single car in the lot. It wasn't Faith's. But it told her that *somebody* was definitely there.

Sabrina parked her bike in the bike rack and chained it up, hanging the helmet on the handlebars.

She tried the door to the arcade, but it was locked. There weren't any lights on inside either. There was a sign hanging in the window that said CLOSED, as if it were just closed for the day and would be opening up again tomorrow, instead of being shut down forever.

Was Faith trapped inside?

Sabrina took a deep breath and let it out. She had to think. The sun was setting fast. She pulled her cell phone out of her pocket and tried calling her sister again. The phone rang in her ear, but she could also hear a distant phone ringing, playing the tinny music that was her sister's ringtone. She held the phone away from her ear and walked through the parking lot until she found a side gate to the park. It was covered with no trespassing signs and heavily padlocked. The fence was chain link, but Sabrina couldn't see through to the other side because green plastic strips had been woven through the links, blocking the view.

The ringtone abruptly stopped.

Sabrina dialed Faith's number again, dread a cold, heavy weight in her stomach. The phone rang again somewhere on the other side of the gate.

She had to get inside.

CHAPTER
FORTY

Sabrina hung up and put her phone in her back pocket. Whoever had Faith was inside Funland. She thought of Mariann Sanchez. The person who had Faith would know what happened to Mariann as well. Sabrina was sure of it. The thought that she might solve this mystery but lose her own sister in the process nearly made her knees buckle.

Sabrina considered calling 911, but then stopped. What would she say? *My sister went on a date without telling me and I'm trying to break in to an amusement park?* Sabrina was so tired of people telling her she was overreacting. She had to see with her own eyes what was really happening. Then she would call.

She backed up a bit and took a running start at the fence, grabbing the top of it and straining until she could pull herself over. It was the most athletic thing Sabrina had ever done, and she silently whooped in triumph even as her muscles screamed from the effort.

She landed on a bed of grass on the other side. Right away she saw Faith's phone on the ground. She grabbed it and tried to scroll through the screen, but the phone was locked. She didn't know her sister's passcode. She shoved it in her other pocket, then stood up straight and took stock of where she was. Jumping the fence had put her on the grass not too far from the go-kart track. To her left was the building that housed the arcade, and to her right was the entrance to the mini-golf course.

There wasn't a soul in the entire place. It felt surreal to be at an amusement park on a Friday evening without any people around. In its prime, it would have been crawling with kids and teenagers. Seeing Funland abandoned like that was eerie with a big side of creepy. No wonder so many kids had liked filming their videos here.

It was getting darker, but Sabrina guessed that none of the floodlights around the park were working anymore. Ominous shadows seemed to grow longer as she stood there. She pressed into one, heart pounding, buying time to think. Faith was here somewhere, but where? Mariann's video had shown her running through trees. An inky line of pines edged the park to the far right, just past the golf course. But the video Faith was in showed her in a building, like a warehouse or something. There wasn't anything like that that Sabrina could see, but just beyond the golf course, nestled amongst the trees, was what looked to be the metal roof of a large outbuilding. It seemed as good a place to start as any.

Sabrina sprinted through the mini-golf course, carefully avoiding the holes and nearly falling into a water hazard before she caught herself. The place smelled of stagnant water, and in the dark, it was too easy to imagine some kind of swamp monster coming up from the mossy depths to grab her. Sabrina hated the dark. She raced through as fast as she could, and a few panicked heartbeats later, she had reached the edge of the tree line.

The chain link that surrounded Funland and separated it from the trees was curiously absent on this side of the park. Here, it was just grass fading into evergreens. Little light penetrated between the trees, and after a few wobbly steps and a near wipeout when her foot came down on a stray golf ball, Sabrina pulled out her phone and used it as a flashlight.

The lay of the land here looked familiar. She was sure she had seen it in one of the videos The space under the trees was dark, and the forest had started to awake with the sounds of the evening: chirping crickets and rustlings that could've been footsteps, or just a squirrel trying to get one last meal before the sun went completely down. Was this the forest where Mariann had filmed her terrified run? It could have been, but it could also be Sabrina's "overactive" imagination jumping to conclusions, which Uncle John had warned about.

"Hello?" Sabrina called into the shadows. It wasn't smart to call out like that, but she didn't know what else to do. If her sister was out here somewhere, she wanted her to know that she had come to help. But there was no answer.

Sabrina told herself that maybe there was a completely simple and logical reason Faith's phone had been on the grass near the gate. What if she and some boy had snuck in here to film their movie, and she had accidentally dropped her phone? It was unlikely, but she clung to that possibility versus the alternative: Someone in Port Riverton really was using Scream Site to kidnap local girls, including Sabrina's sister.

A branch snapped loudly behind Sabrina, and she spun around. "Who's there?"

"Oh, Sabrina. You really should have worked on a different story," came a voice. One that Sabrina knew.

"Mrs. Wembley?" she said.

And then everything went dark.

CHAPTER FORTY-ONE

Sabrina woke on a ratty couch, headachy and nauseous. She could hear the sound of arguing from another room. Sabrina tried to sit up, but her head spun like she was on a roller coaster. She was pretty sure she would puke if she moved at all, so she lay back and tried to remember what had happened.

She'd been looking for Faith, and then she'd heard Mrs. Wembley's voice.

Mrs. Wembley?

Her English teacher was working with Shady99? Why would she help some kind of sick person like that? Or was Mrs. Wembley herself Shady99?

And where was her sister?

"Faith?" Sabrina called out, hoping that one of the arguing voices was hers. A girl suddenly appeared above her and knelt next to Sabrina.

"My name's Mariann. You fell and hit your head. You should take it easy."

Sabrina closed her eyes. That explained the throbbing in her skull. "Your name is Mariann. Is your last name Sanchez?" Sabrina asked through the pounding pain.

"How did you know?" the girl asked, surprise filling her voice.

"Oh my god. I've been looking for you," Sabrina said.

"What? Why?" the girl asked.

"I was trying to figure out what happened to you and some other girls who went missing. I talked to your sister. She's really worried about you." Talking made Sabrina's headache worse, and the more it throbbed, the harder it was to think. But she had to figure out where she was and to find out a way out. She had to find Faith and escape.

"What other girls? You mean Cicely and Rae-Ann?"

"Yes, are they here?" A thrill of satisfaction zinged through Sabrina. Sure, she might be prisoner somewhere and probably had a concussion, but she had been right. Those missing girls *were* caught up in this nightmare too, just as she had suspected! Someone—Mrs. Wembley?—really had been finding girls through Scream Site. Sabrina still didn't understand why, but she felt justified to learn that her instincts weren't off.

But Mariann's next words erased any sense of triumph. "Oh yeah, they're here. Well, Rae-Ann is here. Cicely got tired of making videos and went home a couple of weeks ago." Mariann said, her voice matter of fact. Sabrina realized that for someone who had been kidnapped, she didn't sound too scared.

"Wait, what do you mean she went home? She just picked up and left? Or she escaped?" Sabrina tried to get a better look around. Where was she? Some sort of living room?

"Escaped?" Mariann asked, alarm in her voice. "Why would she need to escape? What are you talking about?"

Sabrina studied Mariann's face. The girl looked just like she had in her final video, but in place of her terrified expression, Mariann now wore one of confusion. Sabrina blinked, wondering if she were imagining it. If Mariann had been kidnapped, shouldn't she be scared and disheveled, like she'd been through some sort of horrible ordeal?

"Where is Faith? Where is my sister?"

Mariann bit her lip. "I think the new girl's name might be Faith. She's probably around here somewhere."

The new girl? Sabrina breathed a small sigh of relief, though she had no idea if any of them were really safe. "I think you're going to have to explain to me what is going on here," she said. "Where are we?"

Mariann smiled. "It's kind of top secret. We work here with Dan shooting videos for a horror movie project that he's working on with the Scarapelli Brothers. I don't know if you've heard of them, but they're really big. Anyway, we're the actors in his movie, but we weren't allowed to tell anyone because of the secretive nature of the project. Dan has this vision. He's going to create what he calls a meta-horror movie, using Scream Site. And part of that vision is to build a lot of hype and drama on the website. He hired us to come work for him—well, he hasn't paid us yet, but he will when he gets paid by the Scarapellis."

Sabrina tried to make sense of what she was hearing. As Mariann chattered on, Sabrina studied her surroundings. It did look like a living room, or at least like a movie set of a living room, with a hall leading to other rooms. And was that a kitchen through that door, where the other voices were coming from?

"Anyway," Mariann went on, "part of the deal was to sort of disappear, and to stop posting our own videos and secretly start working with him on his videos. He wanted people to notice that we had stopped posting. And in his videos starring us, he dropped clues about our identities. Get it? People would get suspicious about the mystery girls in his videos, and that would make them scarier. People post all the time about how real they look! Kind of like the Scarapellis did for *Death Cult*, where they started an Internet rumor to make people believe the film was a documentary rather than a movie, you know?" Mariann stopped gushing. She seemed to have finally noticed the rage on Sabrina's face.

Sabrina was looking at Mariann like she might kill her herself. Sabrina opened her mouth to speak, but nothing came out. Was she dreaming?

Disappointment and embarrassment washed over her. She'd been tricked. She had completely fallen for whatever it was that Mariann had called it, this "meta-horror movie." Here she was, trying to find girls she'd thought were in danger, girls who had gone "missing," only to find out they weren't lost at all.

They were just terrible people.

"Do you know that your sister is worried sick about you?" Sabrina asked, her voice rising in anger.

"She's been to the police and has spent a lot of time searching for you! How could you just do that, take off without letting her know what was going on? How could you be so cruel?"

Mariann leaned back on her heels. "I know. I know this looks bad. But—not that it's anyone's business or anything—Lupe and I weren't exactly on the best of terms when I left. I sort of . . . blocked her messages, because she was totally not supportive of my career. And this was my big break! Trust me, I never would've done it if I hadn't thought Dan's vision was brilliant. I know it might seem like a really selfish thing to just take off like I did, without telling anyone, but I'm getting an incredible opportunity being involved in this project."

Sabrina finally struggled into a full sitting position, ignoring the wooziness that threatened to overwhelm her. She rubbed her head and looked around at the old rundown furniture and tattered rugs. It all looked like it had been rescued from a Dumpster. There was no way this was an official movie set.

"What makes you think the Scarapelli Brothers are actually involved in this project? What do they have to do with this besides owning Scream Site?" she asked Mariann.

Mariann looked like she was excited to spill some gossip. "They're the ones who hired Dan to shoot their film here in Funland for them. Once we have enough footage, they're going to bring in the rest of the production crew. It's going to be amazing."

Sabrina shook her head and then immediately regretted the movement as pain exploded through her skull, blurring her vision.

"It's all a lie," she said to Mariann, speaking slowly to make sure she understood. "There's no Scarapelli Brothers movie here. It's never going to happen. They canceled that movie months ago. And why are you guys hiding out here, completely out of touch with your family for months at a time? Doesn't any of this sound extremely sketchy to you?"

Mariann's expression melted into one of patient indulgence, her smile tight. "No, no, the movie's still happening. See, the Scarapellis just need to find a few financial backers, and then it's going to happen. And the secrecy, well, we're just supposed to sort of lay low, to really stay focused on the project and make sure none of the details leak to the media—and to keep the hype going that's buzzing on the Internet. It's all part of Dan's vision. Just wait. The park is going to be full of cameras, and lights—"

"No," Sabrina said, and something in her voice made Mariann's smile finally disappear. "There is no movie. You aren't going to be famous. Dan Mason has been lying to you."

"What are you saying?" Mariann said, a slight quaver in her voice.

Sabrina clutched Mariann's wrist and said, "I'm saying that whatever is going on here has nothing to do with making a movie, and everything to do with Dan Mason scamming you."

CHAPTER FORTY-TWO

Mariann's expression hovered somewhere between disappointment and disbelief, but Sabrina didn't have time to spell it out for her right now. Mariann's face finally crumpled like she was about to cry, and she fled down a hallway.

Sabrina still didn't know where Faith was, but she knew that her sister would never fall for something as fraudulent sounding as this. A movie project where you ghosted your family, making them think you could be dead? Faith knew just how much pulling a stunt like that would hurt their mother, and after their father's death, Sabrina couldn't believe her sister would ever be so callous or so gullible. Would she?

Sabrina tried to stand. As she did, Mrs. Wembley poked her head through the door from the kitchen. "Sabrina, you're awake! What are you doing?" she asked quietly. "You need to rest. Sit down, relax. You hit your head when you passed out."

Sabrina frowned, because she didn't remember passing out. She just remembered seeing Mrs. Wembley and then everything going dark.

Sabrina was taking in and processing so much information so fast, and she didn't know yet whether she could trust her teacher. What did Wembley have to do with any of this?

"I'm fine," Sabrina said, shaking off Mrs. Wembley's assistance. "I just came here to find my sister. Just take me to Faith, and we'll leave."

Mrs. Wembley gave Sabrina a concerned smile and was about to speak when someone else stepped into view from the kitchen. Mrs. Wembley saw him too and gave a quick shake of her head to Sabrina as she held up her hands ever so slightly. Sabrina got the message: Keep quiet.

The man fixed an icy gaze on Sabrina. She realized in an instant that this was Dan Mason. She recognized him from his photo with the article online. His intense stare slid into a strange smile.

"It's her," Dan said flatly.

"Dan, everything is OK," Mrs. Wembley said quickly. "Sabrina . . . wants to join the project. She's on board, and she's going to convince Faith to stay too."

Sabrina sucked in her breath in alarm. What was Mrs. Wembley saying? Was she insane? Was she working with Dan? But then Mrs. Wembley reached over and softly touched Sabrina's arm. She suddenly understood what was happening. Mrs. Wembley was trying to save her.

Sabrina felt like she was getting whiplash. Was Dan just a scammer, or was he more dangerous than that after all?

"You can convince Faith to stay?" Dan asked, directing his question at Sabrina.

Sabrina fought to stay calm and nodded her head slowly. She wondered if she could discreetly reach into her pocket and dial 911.

"Dan," Mrs. Wembley said, "why don't you go out and get your next scene ready? I'll introduce Sabrina to the others."

Dan looked reluctant but finally nodded. He peered out the window. "Yeah, it's dark now. And we'll want to shoot before the rain starts." Sabrina could see that he was distracted now, thinking about his next video. He grabbed some equipment and started heading for the door. "Will you tell Faith and Mariann to get into wardrobe? And Sabrina too, maybe. I can make the scene work for three. . . . "

Mrs. Wembley told him she would, and Dan headed out the door. As soon as the door closed, Mrs. Wembley said to Sabrina, "Let me help you up. We don't want you to hurt yourself more than you already are. But we have to hurry." She took Sabrina by the arm and guided her down the hallway. In a low voice she asked, "Are you OK, dear?"

"I think so," Sabrina mumbled, even though she had a splitting headache. "Where's Faith?"

"She's back here. She's all right. I'll take you to her," Mrs. Wembley said, but Sabrina noticed that her voice was shaking.

"What's going on? Why are you here?" Sabrina asked. She felt like she couldn't solve one more mystery on her own. She just wanted someone to tell her the answers.

"Sabrina, my brother Dan isn't well. I'm afraid we aren't safe here. We need to call the police."

Dan Mason was Shady99. And Mrs. Wembley was Shady99's brother.

But Sabrina didn't have time to process that. She pulled her phone out and called 911.

CHAPTER
FORTY-THREE

"Sabrina!" Faith yelled and fell into Sabrina's arms the moment she and Mrs. Wembley walked into the room, locking the door behind them. They hugged for a second, but there wasn't time for a proper reunion. They sat down next to each other on a small couch. "Are you OK?" Sabrina asked. "We called the police. They're on their way."

Faith nodded. "Yes, no. I don't know. I am so stupid," she said, dropping her head into her hands. "I thought I was talking to Scott McKenzie online, that cute senior. I thought he was the one messaging me, wanting to make movies. I can't believe I fell for it.

When I got here, that guy Dan said he was a friend of Scott's and that Scott would be here any minute. He convinced me to go ahead and film his video idea while we waited. Since there were other people around, I decided it might be OK. I didn't know what to do. . . . But it was weird. He just wanted me to scream a lot, and then he did a whole bunch of editing on it before he posted it. I never want to make another scary movie ever again!" she said, her voice wavering toward tears.

"It's OK, it's over," Sabrina said, trying to calm her sister down. She hugged Faith again. They would talk about how many stupid things they'd both done later.

Mariann was in the room too, along with a dark-haired girl with big blue eyes that Sabrina recognized as Rae-Ann. She sat on a bunk bed, a magazine open at her side, as she if was at some sort of theatrical summer camp. Were these girls really staying here thinking they were shooting a movie?

"So, you're serious about this? Dan is, like, some kind of fraud?" Mariann asked, arms crossed defensively.

Mrs. Wembley went to the window, watching for the squad cars, and then started pacing back and forth. "Yes, I'm afraid it's true. Dan has had a really tough year. He lost his wife and his business, and it seems he's lost his grip on reality as well. I wish I'd checked on him before now. I suspected he was up to something. I'm so sorry—I should have known. I finally figured out that this is where he's been staying, and I just can't believe—" She broke off, covering her mouth to keep in a sob.

Sabrina took a deep breath and let it out. At last, the pieces began to click together. "How did you think he was a director? Faith, did you believe him?" She looked nervously at the door. How strong was that lock? Would Dan come back before the police got there?

"He's very convincing," Rae-Ann said with a guilty shrug. "At first, I believed him. But then nearly three months passed, and there was still no movie crew, nothing happening, and no paycheck. Just those stupid Scream Site videos that he said were material for the movie." Rae-Ann said. She was barefoot, but a pair of fur-lined boots sat in one corner. Sabrina recognized them from one of Shady99's videos.

It was still sinking in that Dan Mason was Shady99, and even though he hadn't been hurting people in quite the way Sabrina had feared, he clearly was still dangerous.

"He was nice to us, for the most part, and a super talented filmmaker. Our videos got a ton of clicks," Mariann offered, but then she started crying again.

"What about Cicely?" Sabrina asked.

"She got fed up that we hadn't been paid for our work. She left awhile ago. A girl named Georgia left too. She wasn't here very long," Rae-Ann confirmed. "I mean, it's not like he locked us up or anything. . . . He's just really good at persuading people that there's a pot of gold at the end of the rainbow."

Sabrina barely had time to register the fact that Georgia Fanus was involved too, just as she had thought, because right at that moment came a loud *thunk-thunk-thunk* on the door. Everyone in the room froze. Was Dan going to try to break in?

"Open up. Police!"

Sabrina had never been so happy to hear Uncle John's voice in her life.

* * *

"Are you girls all right?" he said, looking around the room. Once the door was opened, Sabrina could hear the hum of other voices out in the hallway, the staticky squawk of a police radio, and uniformed officers moving throughout the space.

Sabrina climbed unsteadily to her feet, then sat back down. "Mostly. But I think I might have a slight concussion," she said.

"Don't move, then. EMTs are on their way." He scanned the room again and took in Rae-Ann and Mariann standing there, looking shell-shocked.

"Looks like I should've listened to you a little more."

Sabrina didn't have anything to say to that. She let out a giant breath that she felt like she'd been holding for weeks, the weight of her investigation and worry finally starting to slip away. She'd been right. There had been something off about Shady99's videos, and someone had been using Scream Site to lure girls into a trap. No one had truly been hurt—not physically, at least—but who knew what Shady99 might have been capable of. How long would it have been before something seriously awful had happened?

While Uncle John checked on Mariann and Rae-Ann, Sabrina held Faith's hand. "Faith, why didn't you run when you discovered what was going on tonight? When you realized it was Dan, not Scotty who asked you to come?"

Faith gave her sister a small, guilty smile. "Because right then I realized that you had been right, or at least partly right. I knew there were other girls here, and I wanted to help them. I figured as brave as you have been all this time, I could be brave too."

Sabrina fought back tears. She and Faith had so much lost time to make up for.

Uncle John reappeared and patted Sabrina's shoulder. He took a deep breath, sank down to his knees next to Sabrina, and pulled her into a hug. "Good job, kiddo. Way to follow those instincts.

I'm sorry I didn't really listen to you. I'm sorry to say I really jumped to the wrong conclusion on this one. I was more worried about getting you to drop something I didn't think was healthy for you to be doing, when I should have listened to what you were actually saying. I'll never make that mistake again." He tugged on one of Sabrina's curls. "But also, if you ever get mixed up in this kind of nonsense again, I will make sure your mom grounds you for all eternity. Got it?"

Sabrina nodded. She had no doubt her sleuthing days were over.

But not her journalism days. She still had a story to write.

CHAPTER FORTY-FOUR

An ice pack and a little pain medicine had done wonders for Sabrina's head. After the paramedics had cleared Sabrina and the other girls, they took them to the station, where Mrs. Sebastian was waiting anxiously for them. After what seemed liked hours of questioning, Mrs. Sebastian was allowed to drive them home. Evelyn, who announced that she was staying overnight to serve them all comfort food and to get the hot gossip, had hot cocoa ready and waiting.

After hugs and tears and a little bit of yelling, the four of them sat at the kitchen table. Faith and Sabrina told their story while Mrs. Sebastian and Evelyn interrupted with questions and more hugs. And repeated warnings from Mrs. Sebastian that they had better never do anything so risky ever again.

It felt good to have everything out in the open. Sabrina realized that the secrets had been eating away at her like acid. She wanted to be all in with her family, and that meant telling one another what was actually going on in their lives. A feeling of hope began to fill the hollow space inside.

* * *

The next day Uncle John came by. "Hey," he said, walking in with fresh pastries. "I thought I'd stop by to tell you that Dan Mason confessed to everything. They've taken him to Forest Valley for psychiatric evaluation."

"What about Mrs. Wembley?" Sabrina asked tentatively. It pained her to think that Mrs. Wembley might somehow be held responsible for her brother's actions.

Uncle John helped himself to the coffee. "She's fully cooperating. She's committed to getting him the care he needs. It's yet to be determined what exactly he'll be charged with. Offering a shady acting gig and persuading people to work for free is a gray area. But posing as someone you're not online is a definite no-no. But then, of course, if Mason truly believed his own lie about working for the Scarapelli Brothers, well, we're probably looking at an insanity plea."

"Kind of sad," Evelyn said, biting into her jelly doughnut. "But still creepy."

"Both true," Uncle John said with a small smile. "A while back the Scarapelli Brothers were supposed to film a movie at Funland. For some reason it fell through. It was a huge blow to Mason. Funland was barely making any money, and he had planned to make all kinds of renovations with the money the film would bring in."

"Not to mention all the business," Faith said. "People love touring movie sets. They would've come from all over to see where a Scarapelli film was shot."

Uncle John nodded. "But, after it was canceled, all those possibilities faded away. Then Mason's wife got sick shortly after—cancer. When she died, he blamed the Scarapellis for her death. He thought if the movie had been made, they would've had the money to go to the doctor sooner, that she would've been diagnosed earlier. He spent a lot of time trying to plan his revenge, and when Scream Site launched, he finally had a way. He'd caught kids filming on his property and decided he should be the one making videos there, not them."

Sabrina picked at her croissant. "OK, I get that Dan conned a bunch of girls into thinking this was some kind of secret project, but why the uniforms?"

"Apparently that was the costume," Uncle John explained. "His movie was about Funland employees being attacked by zombies or something like that. All the girls had to look like they worked there."

Evelyn piped up. "What about Asher3245?" she asked. "What did he have to do with any of it? Why did the IP address point back to Mount Clare? And does this mean that Asher Grey is innocent and I can still marry him?"

Uncle John laughed. "Mason posed as Asher, just like he posed as Scotty2Hotty. He knew Asher since the kid worked at Funland. But Mason also taught wood shop last year at Mount Clare as a substitute teacher, to make money during the park's off-season. He taught a class that Mariann and Asher were both in, apparently, and remembered some pretty specific details that he was able to use to help lure Mariann into his scam. Mason had somehow kept a key card to the school, used the computers there to send some of his messages, and even got a picture of Asher from a yearbook."

Sabrina shuddered to think that Dan had been at their school, poking around in their computer lab and elsewhere. Had he somehow been there that day her printouts had gone missing? "What about the threatening messages that Shady . . . Dan sent to the people with the number one videos?" she asked.

"Well, from what I can tell, he tried to threaten users to take down their accounts if they were knocking him out of first place, but when that didn't work, he switched tactics. That's when he posed as other users, like Scott and Asher. He decided if they were going to make good videos, they should make videos for him," Uncle John said.

"I can't believe I fell for it." Faith ducked her head in embarrassment.

"And poor Lupe," Sabrina said. "Here she was, worried to death about her sister, and this whole time Mariann was just hiding out at Funland, playing Hollywood."

"Some people are willing to believe anything to see a dream come true. I'm sure Mariann really wanted to believe this was her big chance," Mrs. Sebastian said and reached out to squeeze Faith's hand.

"Yeah, I believed those stupid Scotty2Hotty's messages for the same reason," Faith said. "I fell for what he said about making some really killer videos and maybe getting the attention of the Scarapellis. I'm just lucky that Sabrina's reporter instincts were already on the case." She reached over to gently punch her sister's arm.

Sabrina smiled and let Faith's compliment warm her for a moment.

"Well, as we all know, it's been a difficult year. But

I do think we need to have a conversation about this later," Mrs. Sebastian said, giving Faith a meaningful look. "I'm especially interested to hear why you wouldn't ask your mother for permission before going to check out such a thing. Or at least tell someone where you were going. . . . Both of you."

Uncle John cleared his throat. "Well, we're all just lucky that no one was truly hurt. Mariann and the others swear that they were acting the whole time. Dan apparently spent a lot of time watching documentaries about filming horror movies before he started on this, and I think under different circumstances, he really could've had a great film career. Those young women too, with their acting careers, if they could be that convincing. Heck, they still might. Once this story gets out, it might be big enough for someone to contact them." Uncle John set his mug in the sink.

"Oh, and speaking of stories," he said, reaching into his front pocket and pulling out a business card. He slid it across the table to Sabrina. "That's for you. Seems the editor of the *Daily Sun*, Mike Masters, wants to talk to you about writing the article on how this all went down, if you're interested."

Sabrina's eyes lit up. "Uh, yeah!"

Uncle John winked. "Then you should give him a call. Be safe, all of you."

Sabrina walked her uncle to the door to give him

one last hug, and Evelyn headed out too for her shift at Chao's. When Sabrina returned to the kitchen, her mother was gone, but Faith was still at the table, checking her phone. The police had returned it to her after getting the evidence they needed from it.

"Anything new on Scream Site?" Sabrina asked, half joking.

Faith looked up. "Actually, I just deleted the app. Like I said, I don't think I can do scary movies anymore."

"Good call," Sabrina said with a laugh.

"Hey, I never said thanks . . . for being there." Faith trailed off, her expression troubled. "I don't know what would've happened if you and Mrs. Wembley hadn't shown up."

"You're my sister. I'll always have your back," Sabrina said.

Faith smiled and stood. "Dad would be so proud of you, you know? He always wanted us to be able to take care of ourselves. And each other. I'm going to work a little more on that last one." She walked over to Sabrina, enveloping her in a hug. "I love you, Bri."

Sabrina blinked at the nickname, one she hadn't heard since her dad had died. Tears pricked her eyes. "I love you too, Faith."

For the first time in a long time, Sabrina knew everything would be all right.

ABOUT THE AUTHOR

Justina Ireland lives with her husband, kid, and dog in Pennsylvania. She is the author of both full-length books and short fiction and considers words to be her best friends. You can visit her at her website: justinaireland.com.